MURDER BY THE HOLLY
A 1920S HISTORICAL COZY MYSTERY

AN EVIE PARKER MYSTERY
BOOK TWENTY-ONE

SONIA PARIN

Murder by the Holly Copyright © 2024 Sonia Parin

No part of this publication may be reproduced in any form or by any means, without the prior written permission of the author, except in the case of brief quotations embodied in critical articles and reviews. This is a work of fiction. Names, characters, places and incidents are the product of the author's imagination or are used fictitiously. Any resemblance to actual persons, living or dead, organizations, events or locales is entirely coincidental.

ISBN: 9798303977136

CHAPTER 1

Sparkle with Christmas joy

The dining room
Halton House, Berkshire

*E*vie finished her bacon and eggs and drank her coffee. Setting the cup down, she drew in a fortifying breath and, employing her sweetest tone, she said, "A word with you in private, Mr. Winchester."

A cup rattled on its saucer.

Another cup being lifted was stopped midway to its destination, its contents overflowing and spilling.

Cutlery was lowered, and seven pairs of Winchester eyes shifted and turned to look at Evie, the Countess of Woodridge, who sat at one end of the table.

Me? they each seemed to ask.

No one spoke.

Everyone waited.

Evie savored the moment.

Out of the corner of her eye, she thought she saw Brazen Winchester wince, probably because his brother Wilbur had kicked him under the table.

A quick glance to her right provided another display of daring as Theodore Winchester taunted his brother, Clarence, with elbow jabs.

Eugene and Nathaniel Winchester sat opposite each other, both giving their food their full attention. Evie knew it was all an act.

She had been referring to them as the Winchester boys but they were grown men aged in their twenties.

As for Tom Winchester...

Her husband...

Evie gave an impatient shake of her head. "Oh, never mind." Even as she lowered her gaze to her empty plate, Evie sensed all seven pairs of eyes exchanging looks of puzzlement, concern and panic.

Evie looked up and smiled at Edgar who took the prompt to draw her chair out.

"Thank you, Edgar. I'll be occupied in the village for most of the day and will return in time for afternoon tea. I trust all will be well while I'm gone. However, if something should go wrong, feel free to employ whatever means necessary to restore order."

"Very well, my lady."

Avoiding eye contact with everyone sitting at the table, Evie walked out of the dining room and was halfway across the hall when Tom, who had followed her, called out to her.

"Countess."

The edge of Evie's mouth kicked up.

Tom sounded quite cross.

Smiling, Evie murmured, "I wonder what that's about?" Out of the corner of her eye, she saw Holmes appear and stop. The little French bulldog looked at Evie and then at Tom, his little face full of curiosity.

Her smile faded. Lifting her chin and straightening her shoulders, Evie turned to face him and spoke in a calm tone. "Yes, Tom?"

When he spoke, his voice hardened, "What the devil was that all about? You made our guests uncomfortable." His voice rose to a crescendo. "I won't have it."

Oh dear...

"What was that?" he demanded. "So you should be. Just make sure it doesn't happen again. Is that clear?"

Evie pressed her hand to her mouth to stop herself from laughing.

"Yes," Tom continued, "you owe them all an apology. Every single one of them, including me."

Evie lowered her hand, glowered at Tom and then poked her tongue out.

This seemed to confuse Holmes. He took a step toward Evie and then changed his mind and took a step toward Tom. Stopping, he lowered his head and growled.

Tom scowled at him and shooed him away. Taking exception to that, Holmes looked at Evie but she was pretending to hold her ground.

Shaking his little head, Holmes lost all interest in the silly humans and trotted away.

With the rehearsed scene over, she waved and continued across the hall.

When she reached the stairs, she stomped her way up and then along the hallway. Reaching her room, Evie stepped inside and gave Millicent the signal.

Nodding, Millicent slammed the bedroom door so hard, a vase on the mantle teetered and came close to toppling over.

"Well?' Millicent asked. "Did it work?"

Smiling, Evie said, "I won't know until this afternoon."

"And if it doesn't work?" Millicent asked. "Will you then have a proper row with Mr. Winchester, in front of everyone, and with all the servants rushing to eavesdrop?"

Evie doubted it would come to that. In her opinion, her performance had been credible. In fact, if Edgar had been privy to the plan, he might have given her a standing ovation. Then again, Millicent didn't appear to be convinced. "I thought we both put in a good performance. It should suffice. Don't you agree?"

Millicent tilted her head from side to side. "If you ask me, which you did just now, but not when you were planning and plotting…" Millicent stopped to collect her thoughts. "What I mean to say is that if you had asked me, I would have suggested putting on a more dramatic display."

"I'm not sure I follow and how would you actually define a proper row?"

Millicent's shoulders rose and fell. "I think you should have thrown something at Mr. Winchester. Nothing valuable, of course. It's not too late. I could place a few inexpensive items around. You wouldn't even have to aim the vase at Mr. Winchester's head."

Evie conjured the image in her mind and tried to picture the scene. In her first attempt, the vase slipped from her hand. She then tried holding it with both hands but that seemed to ruin the effect. Yes, she would want it to look spontaneous. In her third attempt at imagining the scene, she pictured the vase but the moment she tried to reach for it, it seemed to move away.

"Your face is all scrunched up. You don't seem to like the idea."

"To be perfectly honest, I'm struggling to see myself throwing something at Mr. Winchester. So… let's hope it doesn't come to that. If worse comes to worst, I might have to impose the silent treatment."

Millicent sighed. "As my mother is fond of saying, you should never do anything by half measures."

Evie studied Millicent and tried to penetrate her thoughts. Being quite familiar with her occasional odd behavior, it wouldn't surprise her if Millicent suggested wielding a revolver.

Millicent continued, "If you're going to be bizarre, you might as well be outlandish."

"It's a very fine line, Millicent. If I'm too peculiar, Mr. Winchester might regret ever marrying me."

"I'm sure you jest, milady." Millicent walked across the room and retrieved a handbag from the wardrobe. "If you don't mind me asking, whose idea was it to pretend to have an argument?"

"Mr. Winchester and I tackled the issue at length and we both came to the same conclusion. Guilt would be our weapon of choice." Evie released a long breath. "Actually, it was my idea and I'm inclined to agree it might not have been the best idea, but it was late and we had to do something and... and it was all I could come up with."

"You said you might put Mr. Winchester in the doghouse. How long will he be there for?"

They had discussed their plans the previous evening and, after ironing out all the details of this morning's pretend falling out, they had spent a considerable amount of time negotiating the finer details.

Just how long should they pretend they'd had a disagreement?

Evie had argued against a swift resolution because, in her opinion, that would not guarantee the long-term peace and quiet, not to mention compliance, she sought from the Winchester boys.

Tom had growled and had insisted he would whip them into shape and guilt them into behaving in one day.

Reluctant to end the day on a sour note, Evie had given him until afternoon tea.

She had no idea what he would do to rein in his savage tribe. Evie suspected the task would be made easier if only Tom would stop referring to his kin as savages. Although, she supposed he knew better than anyone what they were like and, more to the point, what they were capable of.

In the short time they'd been in England, they had given Evie a taste of their abilities to disrupt the household with their boisterous games of daring. Evie knew the only solution would be to divide and conquer but they were inseparable. As thick as thieves, she thought, with an uncanny ability to never miss an opportunity to taunt and dare each other into performing the most outrageous challenges.

To think, Tom had assured her she had only ever seen the Winchesters on their best behavior.

A day, Evie thought. Perhaps two…

"We'll see. I suspect the Winchester boys won't be happy about causing a marital rift, especially at Christmas time."

"I heard one talking about knives. Flip blades, to be precise. Although, one of them called it a switchblade."

Alarmed, Evie asked, "Which one?"

Millicent's cheeks colored. "You know I don't like to look at them for too long."

Evie laughed. "Are you afraid they'll charm you?"

Lowering her voice to a whisper, Millicent looked over her shoulder before saying, "They're ever so handsome. Why aren't they married? I mean, they're ever so handsome. They should be married. What's wrong with them? Yes, I've heard Mr. Winchester refer to them as feral, but any good woman would bring them to heel."

"Feel free to try, Millicent."

Millicent gasped. "Don't let Edgar hear you encourage me. It's not just their good looks. They all dress so well. I suppose that means they are wealthy."

Evie knew Tom had helped them, but they'd all managed to carve out their share of successes. "Tom says they do well enough for themselves." Evie smiled because the one time she had asked, Tom had muttered his response and had thrown in a roll of his eyes. She'd known better than to ask for details, however, they'd already shared a few stories about their daredevil schemes, and she suspected those had been quite mild and tame.

Millicent brought out her hat and coat. "I can't believe it's come to this."

"Neither do I, Millicent."

Wilbur and Brazen Winchester had been staying with them for a couple of months and they'd been a handful, keeping everyone in a constant state of suspense, guessing what they would get up to that day.

Their creativity never ceased to amaze Evie. But it put them all on edge.

She had expressed some of her frustration in her correspondence to Phillipa Brady, the Australian playwright who was currently residing in New York, and Phillipa had written back to say she would do everything possible to travel to Halton House just to meet the bunch of *larrikins* because they sounded rather endearing.

Now the other Winchesters had joined them, and every single day had brought a fierce wave of trepidation.

What will they do today?

"I just hope Mr. Winchester sorts them out before Henrietta and the others return from their trip to town."

"I almost forgot." Millicent helped Evie into her coat and smoothed out the collar. "Mr. Holloway's goat has been found safe and sound. He says she must have wandered off and he apologized for any trouble he might have caused."

"I wonder if we'll ever find out what really happened with the goat." Evie had her suspicions, but she hadn't been able to find the proof.

Millicent laughed. "What you really want to know is if there is any way its disappearance can be traced back to us."

That had been Evie's main concern. The fact the

owner had come directly to Halton House to speak with her meant he'd had his suspicions and had already heard about each and every one of the Winchester tribe.

"I'm ready to concede defeat. They're too cunning for me. Especially Nathaniel. He's quiet and contemplative and most likely the leader of the gang."

"You should give him the benefit of the doubt," Millicent suggested.

"What?" Evie turned to look at Millicent. Noticing the delicate tinge of pink on her cheeks, she laughed. "I see. He's the one who's charmed the socks off you."

Millicent lifted her chin. "He's a perfect gentleman. They all are. I've seen how guests behave with housemaids. The Winchester boys are extremely respectful."

"Something tells me the housemaids are disappointed by that."

Millicent grinned.

"You're right, Millicent. They are perfect gentlemen. At least that's something I don't have to worry about."

Millicent's expression changed to a look of puzzlement.

"What's wrong?"

"Nothing really. It's just that... well, as I said, they do always dress well. What was that word you used yesterday?"

"Spiffy?"

"Yes, that's it. They look spiffy. You'd think they'd drive nicer motor cars."

Evie hid her smile as she recalled the day the entire household had been thrown into a state of panic, with everyone rushing outside to see what the commotion was, only to witness a caravan of black motor cars making their way along the drive, one bellowing black smoke, another one with steam bursting out from under the hood, while another struggled to tow a fourth vehicle.

Fixing the vehicles had kept them out of trouble for an entire month.

"They like their Model T motor cars and were surprised to discover them here." Evie adjusted her hat and, as she reached for her handbag, she realized she and Tom had missed something. "Speaking of driving, Tom can't drive me into the village."

"Edmonds can drive you."

Yes, but that meant she'd have to spend the entire day without Tom. Evie grimaced. "Yes, of course. I'm meeting with Mr. Jackson. He's heading the Christmas pageant committee. I've been on edge since you told me he's extremely punctilious."

"I heard that from Anna," Millicent nodded. "She does his house cleaning. I had to wait to return to Halton House so I could look the word up."

"I'm not sure I wish to face Mr. Jackson alone," Evie admitted.

"I don't blame you. I saw him cross the street. A motor car was approaching and, instead of hurrying across the street, Mr. Jackson stopped and glared at the vehicle."

"Heavens. And then what happened?"

"The driver stopped. Then Mr. Jackson adjusted his hat and went on his way, taking his sweet time about it, mind you. Almost as if he wished to make a point." Millicent lowered her voice. "He frightens me. When he walked past me, I swear I stood up straight and pushed my shoulders back." Millicent turned away and threw herself into tidying the room.

Evie searched through her handbag to make sure she had her little notebook and fountain pen. "Millicent?"

"Y-yes?"

"I don't suppose you'd like to accompany me. I mean... you don't really have to, but now that you've acquired your new shorthand skills, you might want to put them to use and take note of what Mr. Jackson says."

Millicent straightened a bottle of scent. Shrugging, she puffed out her cheeks. "Well... If you feel I would be of value."

"Oh, yes. You see, Mr. Winchester usually remembers bits I don't and vice versa. It would be tremendously helpful." And, Evie thought, she wouldn't have to face Mr. Jackson alone.

"Very well. If I must... I mean, if you feel it's absolutely necessary." Millicent's shoulders lowered and she huffed out a breath. "I am your lady's maid and private secretary, so I suppose it goes without saying, but I'll say it anyway. If I must accompany you, then I suppose I will." Millicent looked down at the floor. After a moment of consideration, she smiled and said, "That came out wrong. Of course, what a wonderful... delightful opportunity, milady. Just give me a moment to fetch my hat and coat, and... notebook."

"You're a treasure, Millicent. I don't know what I'd ever do without you."

"You'll never be in that position, milady. Although, there's always Mayberry. I'm sure she'd be only too happy to step in and help out. Perhaps today could be the day."

Surprised, Evie said, "I didn't know Mayberry could take notes in shorthand."

"Well, she can't. I suppose there's not enough time for

her to learn. Perhaps next time." Millicent bit the edge of her lip, almost as if biting the bullet because she knew there was no way out of attending a meeting with Mr. Jackson.

"Cheer up, Millicent. You and I will have lunch in the village."

As Millicent walked away to fetch her hat and coat, Evie thought she heard her murmur, "That sounds like bribery, but I'll take it."

CHAPTER 2

After every storm the sun will smile

The village schoolhouse

During the short drive to the village, Evie did her best to distract Millicent by talking about the preparations for the festive season.

"Phillipa Brady is going to try her best to come. I imagine she will turn her experience into a play. We seem to inspire her."

"I'll let Mrs. Arnold know about Miss Brady's visit. She'll have a room ready for her, just in case, and I know she'll be thrilled to know about us featuring in one of Miss Brady's plays."

Evie had actually been thinking about the Winchester

clan getting up to no good and inspiring Phillipa. She trusted Tom to set them straight. However, she now knew them well enough to know they enjoyed playing to an audience.

When the schoolhouse came into view, Millicent lowered her gaze and slid down in her seat.

Patting her hand, Evie assured Millicent, "Just wait and see. Mr. Jackson will be impressed by your skills."

"So why do you sound worried? I'm sure your voice shook."

"I was just thinking about Mr. Winchester tackling his family. I don't know why, but I just saw us returning to Halton House and finding him with a black eye."

Millicent laughed. "They do enjoy their roughhousing. It's kept us all entertained and it's made Mrs. Arnold's job that much harder as she's been running around keeping an eye on the housemaids. They used to always look forward to their weekly picture shows. Now, I only hear them talking about what the Winchester boys are doing. Mrs. Arnold has to force them to take their half days. They've lost all interest in going out for fear they might miss out on something. When they return from their outings, they're ever so eager to hear of any news to do with the Winchesters."

When Edmonds brought the motor car to a smooth stop outside the schoolhouse, Millicent drew in a breath and stared at the front door while Evie reacted by clutching her handbag.

She'd heard stories about the new school headmaster and Millicent had shared her encounter with the man who had been charged with looking after the local children. The school board had been responsible for engaging his services. She hadn't been present at the interview because it had taken place during the hectic time of her first wedding. Then, she'd been preoccupied with one thing or another, which had included the arrival of Tom's relatives as well as planning her second wedding.

"What time does he expect us?" Millicent asked.

"Eleven," Evie murmured.

Millicent yelped. "We only have five minutes." Pressing her handbag to her chest, she hurried out of the motor car, saying, "Edmonds. Hop to it."

Edmonds promptly jumped out of the vehicle and opened the door for Evie.

"Hurry," Millicent urged.

Reacting to Millicent's panicked tone, Evie scrambled out and just as she was about to set her foot on the ground, she stopped.

What would Henrietta do?

The Dowager Countess of Woodridge would definitely not cower. Indeed, she would rise to the challenge and impose her will by setting the rules of engagement.

Evie drew in a long, calming breath and, instead of rushing out of the vehicle, she tapped her finger against her handbag, the motion acting like a metronome marking her thoughts.

In the years she had been the Countess of Woodridge, she had never pulled rank on anyone and, to this day, she believed her lofty station in life was not something to be abused.

While she had never formed opinions about a person based on someone else's experience, in this instance, Evie decided to rely on her instinct and give credence to the apprehension she felt.

Mr. Jackson would not get the better of her.

They would arrive on time and not a moment sooner.

"Milady!"

Adjusting her gloves and striking an imperious pose Henrietta would approve of, Evie climbed out of the motor car. "Millicent. We have all the time in the world."

Millicent's eyes widened. "No. No, we don't. Not if we know what's good for us."

"Millicent, do please take a deep breath and relax." Evie tried to imagine what Mr. Jackson would be like in person. It didn't take much effort to decide gaiety would be frowned upon. It seemed unfair to jump to conclusions, after all, she hadn't met the man. However, knowing what she did about him, it would be foolish to take any chances and allow him to gain the upper hand.

Millicent took two steps forward and hurried back. "Milady. You're dragging your feet."

"I am not."

"We'll be late. He'll think you're terribly rude."

They walked past the school headmaster's house and reached the entrance to the schoolhouse. Stopping at the gate, Evie searched through her handbag.

"Whatever you're searching for, if you don't have it, I do. Please, milady. Hurry."

Looking up, Evie felt her face drain of all color.

Mr. Jackson stood at the door. He wore a black suit and tie with a pristine white shirt. Evie thought of the people who had interviewed him for the role and decided they must have found him plain, stiff and frosty.

"And quite frightening," she whispered.

At the same time, Millicent whispered, "Perfidious."

Evie looked at her. "Did you say something?"

Millicent leaned in and said, "Perfidious. When Anna described Mr. Jackson as punctilious, I rushed back to Halton House and searched the word in the dictionary. Then I became engrossed and I came across the word perfidious. I'd never heard it before. I wanted to commit the word to memory, so I spent the day composing sentences and including the word perfidious. Even from a distance he looks deceitful and quite untrustworthy." Millicent missed a step. "Oh, dear. I do hope he didn't hear me or, worse, have the ability to read lips. He looks quite stern and disapproving."

"Let's hope he proves us wrong," Evie murmured.

Mr. Jackson remained standing at the entrance to the schoolhouse. Evie didn't wish to cast further aspersions on his character, however, she thought it rather odd that he hadn't taken a single step toward them.

Millicent looked down and whispered, "He's not going to greet us. That's rude."

When they reached him, Mr. Jackson subjected them to a thorough scrutiny before giving a firm nod. "Lady Woodridge."

"Mr. Jackson, good morning." Evie introduced Millicent, although she imagined her trying to fade into the background so Mr. Jackson wouldn't notice her.

"The other committee members are already here. Perhaps we shouldn't keep them waiting any longer."

Millicent coughed.

Evie was certain she did so in order to disguise her opinion.

How rude, indeed.

As Mr. Jackson led the way inside, Evie looked over her shoulder. Millicent was following, albeit reluctantly.

Giving her a nod of encouragement, Evie was not surprised to see Millicent react with a roll of the eyes.

Mr. Jackson walked several steps ahead of them and made no effort to establish a rapport with them.

When he reached the door to the headmaster's office, he stepped aside to let them through, but did not make eye contact.

Evie had never been inside the office, so she took the opportunity to calm her nerves by looking around. She'd hoped to find something to distract her growing concerns but, to her surprise, she found the room practically empty. With the exception of a desk and several chairs, the shelves were bare and the walls devoid of any paintings. Although, the wallpaper showed traces of pictures having once taken pride of place.

"Mrs. Hunter and Mr. Wiltmore arrived punctually." He gestured to the empty chair beside them. That prompted Evie to ask for another chair for Millicent.

Mr. Jackson blinked at Evie and eventually said, "Of course." He then looked at Mr. Wiltmore and signaled to a chair in the corner.

That was enough for Mr. Wiltmore, a member of the school board and a retired country solicitor, to rush to his feet and fetch the chair.

When they were seated, Mr. Jackson rounded his desk and sat down, his back ramrod straight. He then spent a solid minute studying them.

Before speaking, he cleared his throat, "Now that we are all here, I think we should proceed with expediency. I have already delegated tasks for Mrs. Hunter and Mr. Wiltmore. They will report back to me at the end of the week."

Surprised by his militant manner, Evie felt she ought to say something. She knew Henrietta would have used her cane to express her objection and demand a full explanation, after all, they had arrived right on time.

Dismayed by Mr. Jackson's abrupt manner, she did not wish to spend a moment longer than she had to in his presence, so she chose to ignore his rudeness.

Evie turned to smile at Mrs. Hunter and Mr. Wiltmore. They both responded with brisk smiles and quickly looked away.

"As for the decorations," he looked at Evie. "Simple garlands will suffice. There is a hollyhock tree here and at the end of the lane. Also, I am told there are several others to be found in the district. I assume you will know how to find them. I will designate the roles to the pupils and will personally supervise the rehearsals. I believe two will be enough."

Evie leaned forward slightly. "What is the theme?"

It seemed Mr. Jackson would not answer until he'd stared at her for a full minute. "It's the Nativity theme."

"Has the script been written?"

"What sort of question is that? Of course it's been written. Did you not attend Sunday school?"

Despite wanting the unpleasant meeting to be over, Evie asked, "Who decided on the theme? Was it put to the vote?"

"Vote?"

"Last year, we considered several ideas and then put it to the vote. This year, I wanted to propose doing a version of The Wind in the Willows Christmas." Evie glanced at Mrs. Hunter and saw her eyes light up with a look of keen interest. Mr. Wiltmore, on the other hand, gaped and looked as if he wanted the earth to open up and swallow him. "It would be a simple story of Mole and Rat organizing a cozy Christmas for their loopy friend, Toad."

Mr. Jackson frowned. "Why would they do that?" His voice lowered to a menacing growl. "I've never heard of anything so preposterous." He checked his watch and shook his head. "No, it's already been decided." Surging to his feet, he gestured to the door.

They'd been dismissed?

Unceremoniously dismissed?

Without even a by your leave, thank you for attending this meeting?

Evie was about to object when Millicent nudged her with her elbow.

Startled, Evie blurted out, "No, Mr. Jackson, it has not been decided. Not by any stretch of the imagination."

Mr. Jackson's eyes narrowed to slits. "That is your opinion. Mrs. Hunter and Mr. Wiltmore are both in agreement. I believe that is three votes against one." He gave a stiff nod. "Now, if you'll excuse me, I have matters to attend to."

Evie tried to produce a rebuke but everything she wished to say scrambled in her mind and she was left gaping at his back as he made a swift, stiff-necked exit out of the office, with Mrs. Hunter and Mr. Wiltmore scurrying after him.

"How rude." Millicent's eruption echoed in the now empty room.

Jumping to her feet, Evie straightened, lifted her chin, and tried to speak, but again words failed her.

"I think Mr. Winchester will have something to say

about this. You will tell him. Won't you, milady? Yes, of course you must tell him."

"The nerve of the man," Evie finally said.

Echoing her frustration, Millicent roared, "I wouldn't treat a scullery maid with such disdain."

Evie couldn't remember ever feeling so dismayed by someone's behavior. She treated everyone with deference and expected the same in return, and not because she was the Countess of Woodridge. She had been brought up to treat everyone with respect, regardless of their station in life.

"Come along, Millicent. I promised you lunch."

"Lunch? I'm not sure I'll be able to enjoy it. Milady, please tell me you won't let this rest."

"Of course not," Evie grumbled and walked out of the office. When she reached the front door, she made a beeline for the motor car, Millicent following close behind.

Seeing them, Edmonds jumped to attention and opened the passenger door.

Out of the corner of her eye, Evie saw him exchange a raised eyebrow look with Millicent. "Yes, Edmonds, I'm sure you were not expecting us to return so soon."

"Her ladyship is furious and rightly so." Millicent settled in beside Evie. "You would not believe what that Mr. Jackson said. I've never seen such rude behavior, not even when Hilda Brown complained about the butcher shortchanging her on the side of lamb and claiming he'd sold her mutton instead of lamb because the meat had been so tough."

Evie laughed. "Thank you, Millicent. I'm afraid I shall need your help to move on."

"Oh, but you mustn't, milady. On the contrary, you must hold onto your fury and maintain the momentum."

Evie stared wide eyed at Millicent. When she realized Millicent was being quite serious, she laughed again. "Edmonds, please drive on. We're lunching at the tearoom."

"Very well, milady."

Turning to Millicent, Evie smiled. "We mustn't let the man…" She couldn't finish the sentence.

Millicent lifted an eyebrow. "Yes?"

Evie growled. "Give me a moment."

They knew nothing about his circumstances. What if he'd had a bad night? His behavior might have been the result of any number of things beyond his control.

Drawing in a calming breath, Evie tried to employ reason. He'd been dressed in head to toe black. That suggested he might be in deep mourning. Or…

She growled again and decided his black clothes were a reflection of his character.

As Evie fumed in silence, Millicent told Edmonds about the encounter. "Her ladyship had this marvelous idea for the Christmas pageant but he wouldn't hear of it. Can you believe it? He actually said the decision had been made and her ladyship was outnumbered." Sitting back, Millicent said, "Milady, I'd be happy to listen to your idea. It sounds thrilling."

Evie growled. "I'm sorry, Millicent. I can't recall the story. My mind is filled with images of me throttling that man."

Edmonds stopped outside the tearoom. Noticing him looking toward the pub, Evie suggested he might want to have his lunch there and take his time because they were not expected back at Halton House until late afternoon.

Climbing out of the vehicle, Evie took a moment to collect her thoughts. "Once I walk through the door, I will leave all my troubles behind and we can enjoy our lunch and talk about the Christmas celebrations."

"Are you sure, milady? Wouldn't you prefer to discuss the many ways you could make Mr. Jackson pay for his rudeness?"

"To be fair, Millicent, I would need to know if that is his typical behavior."

"It is... I mean, and if it is?" Millicent asked as she pushed the door to the tearoom open.

"Then I would have to question his suitability for the role. I can't imagine how a child could learn under such duress."

Distracted, Evie walked in and collided with Millicent who had stopped midstride.

"My apologies... " Evie looked up and straight at Mr. Jackson who was staring right back at her, his dark look of disapproval prompting Evie to grab Millicent by the arm and drag her out of the establishment.

She did not speak until they reached the motor car and startled Edmonds, who'd been about to set off for the pub. "We have changed out minds, Edmonds."

"You will not believe it," Millicent exclaimed. "There he was, having his luncheon. He told us he had matters to attend to. And now he'll think we're afraid of him. He's all intimidation and no charm."

Evie settled in and closed her eyes.

Why had she fled?

While she accepted full responsibility for her actions,

she couldn't understand why she'd allowed herself to feel so daunted.

"Milady, you mustn't blame yourself."

Evie opened her eyes and stared at Millicent. "What?"

"You're blaming yourself but you reacted to me stopping abruptly. You had no choice."

Evie knew Millicent had just offered her an excuse and she wanted to accept it. But she couldn't.

She had retreated because she'd wanted to avoid an uncomfortable situation. Now she had made matters worse. At some point, she'd have to face him.

Millicent shuddered. "I don't want to wish anyone ill, but if I could make him disappear…"

It took a moment for Evie to realize Millicent had spoken and given voice to her own thoughts.

She looked at her watch. "It's too early to return to Halton House and we all still need to have lunch. Edmonds, please drive us to the next village."

CHAPTER 3

At Christmas, all roads lead home

Halton House

*L*uncheon at a pub five miles away was a lively affair with Millicent doing her best to steer the conversation away from Mr. Jackson. Millicent had judged the mood and had decided it would be best to avoid the subject or risk tempers flaring.

Employing her familiar lively chatter, Millicent talked about all the villagers and their antics, ending each anecdote with a swift assurance that she had heard everything from second hand sources because, of course, she was too busy being a lady's maid and secretary to spend any time gossiping.

Despite the amusing conversation, Evie's mind remained preoccupied with other matters.

Had she made a mistake in not establishing herself as a force to be reckoned with?

Evie knew those would be Henrietta's exact words. That meant she would have to do her best to keep that day's unfortunate encounter to herself. "It should be easy enough." Realizing she'd spoken aloud, she explained, "Mr. Winchester can't know about today."

Millicent agreed. "Not a word to anyone. Although, while I'm not one to impose my will on anyone, if I had to make a suggestion I would say Mr. Jackson deserves to be at the receiving end of your cold shoulder. As for the plain garlands he wants…" Millicent snorted. "I would go out of my way to put together fancy decorations."

"There's nothing I would like better, Millicent. However, in the spirit of Christmas and goodwill to all…"

Millicent huffed out a breath. "Why did I know you were going to say that? I suppose you also wish to lead by example and be perfectly charming, even in the face of adversity. Mark my word, something dreadful will happen to that man. Oh, yes. He will get his comeuppance."

They made their way back to Halton House in relative silence.

Evie gazed out the window. It wouldn't be easy keeping the information from Tom. She told him everything and he never kept anything from her. Well, he had just the one time, but he'd promised never to do it again.

She drew in a deep breath and released a sigh of satisfaction.

Of course, yes, she would tell him about her experience with Mr. Jackson. At least, in a roundabout way.

There was no excuse for Mr. Jackson's bad behavior but Evie couldn't condemn the man before knowing the full story, and she was sure there had to be a story. Perhaps Tom could help her get to the bottom of it.

Looking up, she saw Halton House in the distance and braced herself for whatever was awaiting them. She'd given Edgar instructions and she knew she could trust him to follow them to the letter.

"Have you prepared a story to cover our tracks, milady?"

That hadn't even occurred to Evie. She'd eventually share their experience with Tom but the others were bound to be curious. If for no other reason than to make sure there were no ill feelings. After that morning's charade, they were going to be on their best behavior and engage in polite conversation, which would include asking about her day.

"You could always pretend you're still cross with everyone. Do you think you could manage it?" Millicent smiled and answered her own question. "I doubt it. Knowing you, it would be too much of an effort to pretend to be cross."

"Sometimes I think you know me better than I know myself, Millicent. However, I'm sure I can be vague about our day."

Millicent nodded. "That will work too."

Evie was about to look toward the woods in the distance when she noticed Edmonds shifting and tightening his hold on the steering wheel. Leaning to the side and looking ahead, she understood why he was taking the precaution.

A black Model T was headed toward them at great speed. From a distance, she couldn't tell who was behind the wheel. She narrowed her eyes and tried to see how many Winchesters were in the vehicle.

"Someone's in a hurry," Millicent observed. "If they're not careful they'll run us off the road."

Edmonds took the precaution of slowing down and steered the motor car to the side. The other motor car, however, made no such effort. It continued to career toward them. As the vehicle drew closer, she was able to distinguish the identity of the driver by the way he was hunched over the steering wheel.

Clarence Winchester.

And he wasn't alone.

The passenger appeared to be lounging back, completely unperturbed by the mad dash along the drive.

That had to be Eugene Winchester, who allowed nothing to perturb him.

Evie only had a brief moment to confirm her suspicions when the motor car whizzed by them.

Yes, Clarence and Eugene Winchester.

Millicent swung around to follow the speedy exodus. "Where on earth could they be going in such a hurry?"

While Evie asked, "What are they rushing away from?"

With any luck, Evie thought, they were about to arrive in the midst of a chaotic scene and no one would think to ask about their wretched day.

Swinging back, Millicent looked toward the front entrance to Halton House and gasped. "Milady! Is Mr. Winchester wielding a rifle?"

Good heavens!

Was he?

Tom and the remaining Winchester boys were all outside, standing near the front entrance.

Edmonds slowed down and stopped. "My lady, would you like me to offer Mr. Winchester my assistance?"

Assistance? In what?

Herding the Winchester boys?

Evie couldn't blink. Millicent had been wrong. Tom wasn't holding a rifle. Tom stood facing the front door, while the four Winchester brothers stood with their backs to the door. Every time one took a step, Tom cracked the bullwhip he held.

"Thank you, Edmonds. I believe Mr. Winchester has everything under control." She didn't wait for Edmonds to open the passenger door. Jumping out of the vehicle, she approached the scene with caution. "Tom!"

"Not now, Countess. I've already lost two of them, I need to herd these lot back inside."

Brazen tried to confuse Tom by pushing Wilbur and making a run for it in the opposite direction but Tom was too quick. He cracked the whip and stopped him in his tracks.

"One more step and I'll take the tip of your nose off," he warned.

Evie was about to speak up when Edgar appeared from around the corner carrying a hunting rifle.

Instead of being curious about the need for such measures, Evie wanted to know how Tom had come by the bullwhip. Had he armed himself with it so he could keep the Winchester boys in check? And why had the other two escaped?

Millicent sidled up to Evie and whispered, "Milady, are you going to stop Mr. Winchester?"

Tom cracked the bullwhip again and all the Winchester boys jumped back a step.

"Follow me, Millicent." Lifting her chin, Evie walked straight toward the front door, saying, "Don't let us interrupt you." She then turned to the butler. "Edgar, some tea, please."

When she reached the first step, she stopped and, looking over her shoulder, thought to add, "Everyone. Inside. We are going to have afternoon tea like a normal family."

She walked in and whispered, "Are they following?"

"Yes, milady. But they don't look happy about it." Millicent helped her out of her coat and took her hat and bag. "I'll take these up. I suppose I'll hear about it all later on."

"Don't be silly, Millicent. Hurry back. You don't want to miss the show." As she turned, Evie gasped. "Good heavens!"

Her eyes widened and she swept her gaze around the large hall. There were usually several chairs arranged in front of the fireplace. Two of them had been toppled over and the cushions strewn about. Evie's eyes flew to the display of antique swords. Thankfully, they were all still in place.

"There must have been quite a scuffle here," Millicent said and dashed away, adding, "please don't start without me."

Evie walked into the drawing room and went to sit by the fireplace, her focus on that cup of tea that would restore her.

She lounged back, her hand resting on the armrest. The day had started well enough. She and Tom had spent days discussing his relatives and their antics. Then, the previous evening, they had worked on a perfect plan to bring them to heel. They'd known it would take too long to tackle them individually. The plan to make them think they were responsible for causing a rift had been perfect. Tom had assured her they would then become their brother's keeper, each one keeping the other in check.

Something had definitely gone wrong.

One by one, the Winchester brothers walked in looking rather glum. Evie couldn't even begin to imagine what she'd interrupted.

They had definitely been up to something. A rebellion of sorts. She hoped it hadn't been a mutiny against Tom.

Evie decided it must have started with one of the Winchester brothers standing up to Tom, with the others then following and working in tandem.

Clarence and Eugene had managed to escape.

Had one of them been the first to act or had they both taken advantage of someone else's pluck?

Her money would be on Brazen Winchester. Yes, out of all the Winchester brothers, he was always the one to lead the others in all manner of tomfoolery.

Evie would never forget the apple shot he had taunted Tom into participating in. A great deal of thought had gone into it and, fortunately, she had managed to interrupt proceedings before anyone could be seriously injured.

Finally, Tom entered, still holding the bullwhip and sporting a dark scowl.

Two footmen arrived and set trays of tea and food on

a long table. They were followed by Edgar who still carried the hunting rifle.

When Millicent appeared at the door, her cheeks were flushed and she was trying to catch her breath.

Evie stood up and walked to the table to pour herself a cup of tea. When Tom joined her, she smiled. "How was your day?"

His eyebrow quirked up and he whispered, "Is it true?"

Tilting the teapot to pour her tea, she asked, "Is what true?"

"Did you argue with Mr. Jackson?"

Evie looked up, her eyes wide with surprise. "How—" she broke off and yelped when she realized her teacup had overflowed.

Edgar rushed to assist, moping up the spillage with discretion and ease.

Lowering her voice, Evie asked, "How did you hear about that?"

"So it's true."

How on earth had the news spread and reached Halton House so quickly? Granted, they had driven to the next village and had sat down to a leisurely lunch in order to avoid arriving at the house too early. Had that been enough time?

"Who told you?"

"A footman heard it from one of the housemaids who heard it from a delivery man."

Evie stared at him. "And? Whom did he hear it from?"

"Countess. How am I supposed to know. I was merely trying to make a point. Word spread from person to person and finally reached us."

"And does that explain the bullwhip you're still holding?"

"I confiscated this from Brazen."

Brazen!

She'd been right.

Evie considered all the reasons Brazen might have wanted a bullwhip. Assuming he had come into possession of it for the express purpose of arming himself, she asked, "What did he plan to do with it?"

Tom smiled. "Did you just consider the many reasons he might have come up with to justify resorting to the bullwhip?"

Evie nodded.

"And you decided to skip past the obvious ones and ask me? Any one of the reasons you imagined could be applied to the circumstances."

Tom challenged her to impress him.

"Very well…" Under normal circumstances, Brazen might have wanted to perform a circus trick or some sort of test of skills. However, she had found everyone outside and two of the Winchester boys had already made their escape."I employed deductive thinking. I arrived and found everyone outside and you trying to corral them. I'd already encountered Clarence and Eugene on the road, and then assumed the others were trying to make their escape. And now I'm thinking they all wanted to go to the village and have a word with Mr. Jackson." Or worse, she thought. Teach him a lesson.

"Impressive."

Evie looked past his shoulder and murmured, "Is Edgar under orders to shoot?"

"Yes. You gave him permission."

"I never imagined he would take such extreme measures."

Tom set his bullwhip down and poured her another cup of tea.

"Oh, dear. Shouldn't you rush out and stop Clarence and Eugene?"

Tom shrugged. "They won't get far. Yesterday, I asked Edmonds to siphon the fuel and leave only just enough for them to drive up to the gate."

"What? Why did you do that?"

"To limit how far they can travel away from the safety of the house. If you heard half the things they get up to in the village… The less said, the better."

Evie looked into her cup of tea. She'd often heard Henrietta claim tea was quiet wisdom in a cup. "What exactly did the footman say he heard?"

"Mr. Jackson was extremely rude to you and you tried to put him in his place."

She had tried and failed. "Actually, I tried to reason with him." And then she'd issued an ultimatum.

There had only been two witnesses.

Mrs. Hunter and Mr. Wiltmore.

Had one of them spread the rumors or had someone else been hovering within hearing?

Tom leaned in and whispered, "Retribution."

Before he could explain, Brazen approached. "Cousin Evie, on behalf of everyone, meaning, myself and my brothers, I would like to say we are at your disposal. Just say the word and we will extract a full apology from that scoundrel, Mr. Jackson. Someone has to think of your honor." Brazen gave Tom a look that spoke of unresolved issues and resentment. Clearly, the statement did not include Tom.

"Thank you, Brazen, but that won't be necessary. I can deal with him. In fact, he already knows where I stand."

"Well, it's just not right."

Nathaniel, the ruminating Winchester, boomed, "Well, it's just not right."

Wilbur and Theodore both agreed and echoed the sentiment.

A heated discussion erupted among them, each one contributing their idea of how they would exact retribution from Mr. Jackson.

Tom smiled at Evie. "I told you. Retribution."

Sounding worried, Evie asked, "How determined are they?" Evie shot the bullwhip a quick glance. "Never mind." She'd seen the proof for herself. "Out of curiosity, did you have to wrestle someone to get that bullwhip?"

"Yes, you should be impressed. It was one against six. I didn't want to get the footmen involved and Edgar had already raced off to get the rifle."

Evie closed her eyes and took a long sip of her tea. For that brief moment, she imagined calm had been fully restored. Then she opened her eyes and looked out the window.

Tom followed her gaze and they both saw one of the Model T vehicles the Winchester boys had acquired rolling along the drive.

Clarence Winchester sat behind the wheel while Eugene Winchester pushed the vehicle.

"They got further than I expected," Tom said.

Meanwhile...

At the local railway station

Sarah shrugged, "No one is answering."

"Nonsense," Henrietta declared. "Operator, try again."

"She's no longer on the line."

"Tell her to get back on the line."

"Henrietta, it doesn't quite work that way and, besides, she's already tried twice before. This would be the third time, so we've exhausted our chances."

Staring at Sarah, Henrietta scoffed, "What sort of reasoning is that?"

"Practical reasoning."

"Did you tell her the number belongs to Halton House?"

"Mrs. Clifton knew, Henrietta."

"You know she has a nervous twitch. Perhaps she made the wrong connection."

"She said the phone is on another call or disconnected."

"But that's impossible. What is the point of having the contraption if we can't get through? Also, there are several telephones at Halton House. Are you telling me not one of them works?"

"Henrietta, there might be several telephones but they are all connected to the same line."

"That's absurd. What a silly notion."

Toodles, who'd been standing by ready to intervene, said, "We should send someone to Halton House."

They all turned to the station master who had been listening to the conversation.

When he looked away and tried to look busy, Henrietta tapped her walking cane. "This fine gentleman will assist us."

A crisp voice erupted, "He has done all he can to assist us by allowing you to use the telephone. Now step aside."

They all turned. Sarah looked apologetic. Toodles smiled in surprise, while Henrietta scoffed and delivered her best look of defiance.

Lifting her chin, Henrietta stared at the man. "How dare you."

Ignoring Henrietta, the man pushed past her and addressed the station master. "I believe a parcel has arrived for me. It's addressed to Mr. Jackson."

He never saw the blow to his head coming.

The drawing room, Halton House

Clarence Winchester walked in, his hands in his pockets, his hat pushed back, and a toothpick poking out from the corner of his mouth. His brother Eugene walked several steps behind him, kicking at an imaginary can, his lips pressed, his eyes drawn down into slits.

Neither one spoke as they approached the table and helped themselves to tea and fruit cake.

The others watched them and Brazen was the first to speak. "How far did you get?"

"Not far enough," Clarence replied in a gruff tone. "Apparently, there's a shortage of fuel. We just spoke with Edmonds and he said the delivery is late."

Eugene tipped his head back. "We filled up the day

before in the village but the tank was running on empty. Guess it must have a leak. Either that or…"

They both looked at Tom.

Clarence nodded. "We might have bad news for you, Tom. It's possible you have a fuel thief. But never fear, we'll get to the bottom of it."

They both spent the next half hour talking about their determination to get to the village and how the motor car had become sluggish, laboring up the slope and then speeding out of control down the slope, only to then run out of steam.

"We had to push it all the way back."

"Not we," Eugene interjected. "Just me. And the worst part was that man who refused to help us. He drove right by us. We'll be hunting him down tomorrow to teach him a lesson in manners. Although, Clarence reckons he might have been on his way to a funeral because he was dressed all in black."

Oh, dear heavens. Not Mr. Jackson…

Evie wanted to ask Eugene to describe the man. She set her cup down and, looking out the window, she gave it some thought. They didn't appear to be acquainted with Mr. Jackson, otherwise, they would have recognized him.

Deciding it would be best to change the subject, she turned to smile at him only to stop and look out the window again.

Not believing what she was seeing, she rounded the table and walked toward the window for a closer look.

"What is it?" Tom asked.

"It's a horse drawn cart carrying bales of hay and… Good heavens. Henrietta, Sarah, and Toodles."

CHAPTER 4

Not a creature was stirring, not even a mouse

The next morning

*E*vie chose to have breakfast in bed and managed to get through her first cup of coffee before Millicent burst in.

"Milady, are you ill? Why are you still in bed? You never have breakfast in bed."

"There's always a first time, Millicent. I rang the bell and when one of the housemaids appeared, I made the decision to indulge." Something she would not have done if Millicent had come. "Could you bring out my walking shoes, please? I'd like to spend the morning collecting the holly for the garlands. The sooner I accomplish that task, the sooner I can be done with Mr. Jackson." Evie stifled a groan. She didn't want to go anywhere near the schoolhouse, but the tree there would provide a sufficient supply for the garlands. She knew holly could be found somewhere on the estate but that would involve trudging through the woods and she didn't want to stay away from the house for too long.

"Why don't you get one the housemaids to collect the holly and make the garlands?"

"Because I was charged with the task."

Millicent chortled. "You're afraid Mr. Jackson will find out and think you're too posh to roll up your sleeves." Before Evie could respond, Millicent added, "My apologies. That was an unfair observation. You did your best to stand up to him. Anyhow, her ladyships and Toodles made a special effort to get up and go down to breakfast. They were expecting to find you in the dining room. I believe they are still expecting your presence."

"And what took you so long to come up and tell me?"

Millicent became intrigued by the shoes she'd brought out of the wardrobe.

"Millicent?"

"I happened to overhear a conversation and I had to hear the entire exchange so… so I could tell you about it without leaving any details out." Satisfied with her response, Millicent set the shoes down and turned her attention to selecting an outfit for Evie.

"And?"

"And what?"

"What did you overhear?"

Millicent took a moment to consider her response before saying, "Edgar told a footman it was now his duty to make sure the telephone was always working. You see, when the news about your clash with Mr. Jackson reached the house, everyone had been in the library. The Winchester lads wasted no time in deciding they needed to redeem your honor. That's when Mr. Winchester tried to stop them and he had to tackle a couple of them. Edgar thinks someone bumped against the desk and the telephone became disconnected. He didn't notice it because the skirmish moved out into the hall. If you recall, there were chairs turned over. Anyhow, that's why their ladyships and Toodles couldn't get through when they telephoned from the railway station and had to settle for the first available transport they could find, which happened to be a horse drawn hay cart."

Evie remembered asking why they hadn't been able to get through on the telephone but then Henrietta had commandeered everyone's attention with one of many tales about their travels in town.

Throughout dinner, Henrietta had continued to regale everyone with her amusing tales and Evie had been only too happy to put that day behind her.

"Did you happen to eavesdrop on what Henrietta was saying at breakfast?"

"Not deliberately." Millicent grinned. "Her ladyship is still talking about the trip to town. If I didn't know better, I'd think she's trying to hide something but I can't imagine what that might be. Her ladyship is not one to keep secrets. At least, I don't think she is."

"Henrietta is probably trying to steer the conversation away from the gifts she purchased," Evie suggested. "She always has a grand time finding just the right Christmas gift for everyone. Something perfectly useless but quite amusing. Last year, she gave away so many hints, everyone knew exactly what they were getting a week before Christmas." Evie put her tray to one side and jumped out of bed. "I think I heard enough tales yesterday and last night. Going out to collect some holly will be my excuse for missing out on the rest of her adventures. Edmonds will need to know and... I'm thinking we should leave by the back door."

An hour later...

Evie and Millicent used the back stairs to make their way out of the house. Edgar had been assigned the task of delivering a note to Tom explaining their absence and had been given explicit instructions to hand over the note after they had made their getaway.

Millicent had not questioned Evie's tactics and Evie wondered if she should be concerned about Millicent's easy acceptance of her scheme.

They walked out into the cobblestone yard and dashed toward the waiting motor car. While they encountered several footmen and housemaids along the way, not a single one showed the slightest interest or curiosity about their odd behavior.

As they settled into the back seat, Evie looked toward the stables and saw a cart full of hay being unloaded. Laughing, she shook her head. She would never forget the sight of the dowagers and Toodles riding in the back of the cart, rugged up in their winter coats and holding on for dear life.

Edmonds drove out of the yard but, instead of heading toward the front of the house, he drove around it and took a side road.

Millicent leaned in and whispered, "I told Edmonds to avoid detection, milady."

"Good thinking, Millicent."

"I fetched this morning's post for you, milady, but only the interesting letters. There's one from Caro… I mean, Lady Evans. I hope she hasn't changed her mind about coming here for the festive season."

Evie took the envelope. As she removed the sheath of paper from it, she said, "I wonder why they didn't organize another mode of transportation. There's always a young lad hovering around. They could have sent him to the pub to ask if anyone had a motor car and was willing to drive them or…" She looked up. "They could have asked someone to drive to the house and deliver a message."

Millicent stared at the letter. After a moment of silence, she looked up. "Did you actually want me to answer?"

"What? Oh… Well, if you had an idea. Yes."

"I assume you're referring to the dowagers and Toodles."

Evie nodded.

"I don't have an answer. Other than the obvious one. You weren't there to make the suggestion. Also, they were probably weary and wanted to get back as soon as possible."

"In a hay cart?" Evie laughed. Shaking her head, she

turned her attention to the letter. "You can rest easy, Millicent. Caro will be arriving as promised. Her mother in law has actually traveled to Paris and will be spending Christmas there with friends. Caro mentioned something about her going there to prepare for an exhibition of her paintings in the new year."

Finishing the letter, Evie again turned her thoughts to the dowagers and Toodles. It really seemed odd for them to have traveled the way they had. Not only that. She found Henrietta's behavior unusual. Or, rather, more unusual than usual.

"Millicent, you might be right about Henrietta hiding something from us. I just can't imagine what it might be."

Millicent's distracted nod prompted Evie to ask, "What's wrong?"

"Nothing really. Except…" Millicent signaled ahead. "As we get closer to the village, I can't help giving in to a feeling of dread."

"Why?"

"What if we encounter Mr. Jackson?"

Evie looked out the window. "Where else can we get some holly from? I know there's some on the estate, I'm just not sure where."

Perking up, Millicent said, "On the edge. There's a well trodden path because people use it to cut through and I've heard some go hunting around for pine cones. Which isn't a crime. Not like poaching. I mean…"

"I think I know what you mean and, if it'll make you happier, we could try our luck."

Millicent wasted no time. Leaning forward, she directed Edmonds to turn back. "You'll have to wait by the side of the road. Her ladyship and I will walk the rest of the way. It's not far." Millicent sat back and grinned. "I brought a large basket to carry the holly."

"Just as well I put on my walking shoes and rugged up," Evie mused. "By the way, Caro sends her regards and says she's looking forward to seeing you again."

After a short drive, Edmonds steered the motor car off the road and edged his way close to the path.

Pulling on her gloves and pushing up her coat collar, Evie stepped out of the motor car and looked up and down the road. "I never think about it, but I realize now I could easily become the subject of people's dinner table conversation."

Millicent laughed. "Do you really think people weary from their day's labor would bother to talk about you?" Clearing her throat, she deepened her voice and said, "You'll never guess, so I'll tell you. I saw her ladyship from the big house trudging along the path. She wasn't alone. She had that nutty lady's maid with her. They were up to no good. I'm sure we'll hear all about it tomorrow."

Evie blinked. After a lengthy pause, she laughed. "I thought I might need to explain why I thought I'd be talked about, but it seems you know me too well."

Millicent brought out the basket and held up a small pruning shear. "The gardener made me promise I wouldn't lose them. Heaven help me if I do."

As they walked along the narrow path, ducking in places to avoid overhanging branches, they picked up any pine cones they came across and chatted about the Christmas preparations.

"Here's one." Millicent stopped by a holly bush and got the pruning shears. "With or without berries?"

Looking down the path, Evie saw another bush. "Both,

I think. But not too many. There's another bush further ahead." She took the basket and held it out for Millicent to fill. "We can add some red ribbon to make it really pretty and maybe some oranges and pine cones."

Reaching the next holly bush, Millicent studied it to make sure she didn't take too much from one side. "I don't want to leave it looking scrawny." Studying the branch, she paused. "I think it might actually be a good idea to go to the schoolhouse and get some from there too. You don't want Mr. Jackson to think you're frightened of him."

"Do we really care what he thinks?" Evie studied the bush and reached for a branch, holding it so Millicent could cut it. Before reaching for the next one, she stepped back for a better look. To her dismay, her foot stepped on something and she suddenly lost her balance and fell backward.

"Milady!" Millicent dropped the pruning shears and propelled herself forward, yelping, "Oh. Oh…" Her yelp turned into a shriek. "Oh, my goodness."

"I'm fine, Millicent. At least, I think I am."

Millicent's eyes were wide and her face had paled.

"What is it? Did I fall on something horrid? Am I going to smell all the way back to the house?"

For once, Millicent couldn't get any words out.

Evie scrambled to get up. As she propped herself up, her hand came into contact with something solid yet soft. "Oh." She closed her eyes. "Please tell me it's not an animal." Recovering from her initial shock, she now realized she'd landed on something fleshy.

A sheep? A cow? A deer?

Millicent gave a vigorous shake of her head. Finding

her fortitude, she reached down, grabbed hold of Evie's arm and, with a loud grunt, hauled her up.

Evie brushed the palms of her hands against her coat and turned to see what she'd fallen over.

Her eyes landed on a pair of black shoes. Shoes attached to feet... to legs...

A body?

"Oh... Dear heavens."

"He's obviously dead," Millicent whispered. "You fell on him. If he'd been alive, he would have said something." She leaned forward and raised her voice. "Hello? You there, are you alive?"

"What are you doing, Millicent?"

"Making sure he's dead. Or, rather, making sure he's not hanging on by a thread and having to suffer through my nonsense."

Collecting her thoughts, Evie said, "Millicent, run and tell Edmonds. We're closer to the house than the village. He needs to go there and... and tell Mr. Winchester to contact the police."

"Before we know if he's really dead?"

Evie growled. Clenching her back teeth and curling her fingers into fists, she surged forward and bent down.

"Milady, I would have done it myself... but you didn't ask and I didn't wish to presume. Of course, I'm glad you thought of doing it instead of asking me. It's something I wouldn't wish on anyone..."

Evie scooped in a breath and pressed her fingertips to the man's neck. She'd intended searching for a pulse but she knew straightaway there wouldn't be one.

He was stone cold... *dead.*

"Are you going to turn him over? I wouldn't. You don't

want that image stamped in your mind, milady. You've done enough." Millicent stepped forward and drew Evie back. "I hope I'm not overstepping, but I think you need help tearing yourself away from... the scene."

Good heavens.

They were standing right in the middle of a crime scene.

Straightening, Evie looked at the ground around them. Their steps hadn't left any indentations on the ground.

"Milady?"

"Go. Go tell Edmonds. Hurry, Millicent."

"And leave you here alone? I'm not sure I can do that, milady. If anything were to happen to you, I'd never hear the end of it, and I'd have to suffer Mr. Winchester's wrath, as well as all the other Winchesters' wrath. Even if they don't say anything, I'll know they'll be thinking how disloyal I was for leaving you alone."

"Millicent, are you in shock? Do I need to shake you?"

Millicent bent down, picked up the pruning shears and gave them to Evie. "In case you need to defend yourself." As she dashed away, she called out over her shoulder, "I'll be as quick as I can be."

Evie nodded without quite knowing what she was agreeing to. Her eyes felt gritty from staring at the body without blinking. Inhaling, she once again looked at the ground around her.

Nothing stood out. Then again, she did not have a trained eye for such things. Regardless, it hadn't rained in day so the ground was dry.

Sweeping her gaze around, she did her best to avoid looking at the body. She'd already seen more than enough.

It was a man in a black suit.

What were the chances?

No, it couldn't be Mr. Jackson.

Evie thought she'd noticed his arms stretched out by his sides. If she wanted to make sure, she'd have to look again.

"What's keeping Millicent?" she murmured and pushed herself to look.

Yes.

His arms were stretched out by his sides.

"How odd." A moment earlier, when she'd stumbled, her arms had flapped around and then instinct had told her to brace her fall.

He was face down and his arms were by the sides of his body. He can't have fallen, she thought.

Evie looked along the narrow path but didn't see any sign of Millicent.

Leaning forward, she noticed the man's suit jacket was higher than it would have been if he'd been standing up.

Shooting the path another quick look, she then took a step closer to the body.

She was about to take another step when she heard the pounding of footsteps, so she stepped back.

"Milady! Milady!" When Millicent reached her, she took a moment to catch her breath. "Thank heavens. You're alive. I know it was a silly thought but we already have one dead body and we don't know how long it's been there." She signaled toward the road. "Edmonds rushed off to get help and, if he knows what's good for him, he'll be rushing straight back."

"Thank you, Millicent."

Noticing the basket on the ground, Millicent reached

for it and jumped back, almost as if she didn't want to get closer to the body than she absolutely had to. "What do you think happened?"

Evie handed Millicent the pruning shears. "I have no idea."

"He might have wondered off the road," Millicent suggested. "Maybe he had too much to drink. Yes, he had too much to drink and lost his way and stumbled and fell... on his face. Oh..."

"What?"

"Does it look like he might have fallen on his face? I think if I fell on my face, I'd try to break my fall. Look at his arms. They're by his sides. I might be wrong. I knew a lad who could just topple over like a felled tree. He used to entertain us by slipping his hands in his pockets and just falling. We all thought it was hilarious. Don't mind me. I'm just blabbering. I mean, it's not every day you see a dead body. Although, we've had more than our share. You in particular have seen more dead bodies than I hope to ever see in my entire lifetime. Funny about that. Women in my family live to a ripe old age, and I always think I'll live to a ripe old age, but you never know. If one thing doesn't get you, something else might. I should avoid walking along paths in the forest."

Evie reached for Millicent's hand. "They'll be here soon."

"If you don't mind, I'll just keep babbling because I really need to get to the burning question. Is it Mr. Jackson? Oh, that just came out. I actually meant to lead up to it. Of course, it's hard to say because he's face down, but I have a feeling it is him. And, if it is him, how are we going to explain finding his body? The police are going to want to know and we'll have to tell them we were collecting holly for the garlands and we were getting it here because we didn't want to get it from the schoolhouse and that's when, if they're good at their job, they'll ask why we didn't want to get it from the schoolhouse and one thing will lead to another and they'll find out about your clash with Mr. Jackson and they'll look at you with suspicion… Ouch, milady, you're squeezing my hand."

Evie released Millicent's hand. "Here they come."

Millicent rubbed her hand. "Thank goodness."

CHAPTER 5

Don't get your tinsel in a tangle

Halton House

*E*vie had insisted on returning to the house, but the moment it came into view she wished she'd had the resilience to stay and wait with Tom for the police to arrive.

"It was very kind of Mr. Winchester to ask how you were and then turn to me and ask how I was. It shows he has his priorities straight and is also considerate of others. In hindsight, I'm thinking we were lucky to come across the body because you knew what to do. Anyone else might have been frightened for their lives and run off without informing the authorities. It might have been days before the body was discovered and, by then, it would have been a horrid sight, mangled by wild beasts and ravenous birds of prey."

Smiling at Millicent's vivid imagination, Evie patted her hand. "As soon as we arrive, we'll have a nice cup of tea and try to put the experience behind us."

"That's not likely to happen anytime soon. The police will want to speak with you."

Right at that moment, that was something Evie didn't wish to think about.

"What are you going to tell the others? I'm surprised the Winchester lads didn't come with Mr. Winchester." Millicent leaned forward. "Edmonds, do the others know?"

The chauffeur shook his head. "Edgar delivered the message and I asked him to be discreet about it and only tell Mr. Winchester."

Satisfied with the response, Millicent sat back. "We're about to arrive. You'll need to think fast, milady. Even if they don't know what's happened, they are bound to be curious. They have a knack for noticing the strangest little details. Every morning, they all turn up at the breakfast table and make sure to check they are not wearing the same colored tie. Woe to anyone who is because they are sent off to change it and that's when they play a prank and one of them will produce a tie to match the color of the one… I've lost my train of thought, but I'm sure you know what I'm talking about."

"I do and, as for what we'll say to them, I think it might be best to play it by ear. Everyone must be busy with their morning's activities. With any luck, they didn't even notice Mr. Winchester leaving."

Edgar must have seen the motor car approaching. He stood at the door and, as soon as the vehicle stopped, he hurried to open the door.

Walking toward the front door, Evie asked, "Do the others know, Edgar?"

"No, my lady. Lady Sarah was the only one around and she happened to be crossing the hall when Mr. Winchester left, but she didn't ask any questions."

That could be a problem, Evie thought. Sarah might not have been curious, but she was bound to mention Tom's departure to Henrietta, and she would definitely wonder about it.

Edgar cleared his throat. "Edmonds mentioned something about you finding a body, but he didn't have any details. Mr. Winchester telephoned the constabulary and was told they would be there in under an hour."

Evie drew in a calming breath and tried to prepare for whatever was about to unfold. Millicent was right. The police would eventually find their way to the house because, of course, they would want to speak with her.

Edgar took the initiative and said, "When Edmonds came with the news, the Winchester brothers were not in the house. Straight after breakfast, they all made their way to the stables and have been quite busy working on their vehicles and, dare I say, staying out of Mr. Winchester's way."

"That's a relief," Millicent said and went on to explain, "we were worried the Winchester lads might rush off and cause some sort of havoc. There's going to be plenty of that soon enough. I'll go in and get the tea ready, milady. I assume you'll be headed for the drawing room."

Evie looked at Edgar. "Is anyone else in there?"

Edgar nodded. "Lady Henrietta has been busy with her correspondence."

Evie considered avoiding Henrietta and heading straight for the library. While she would prefer to contain the situation and not tell anyone for a while longer, she changed her mind and decided it would be easier to share the news, at least incrementally, and Henrietta would be a good starting point.

She turned to Millicent. "I'll be in the drawing room and you might want to join us with your notebook, please. I'll need to keep track of what I say."

After removing her hat and coat, Evie headed straight for the drawing room.

She found Henrietta sitting at the escritoire, her pen flying across the page. Not wishing to interrupt her, Evie went to stand by the window and waited for Henrietta to finish writing her letter.

"Evangeline! We all missed you at breakfast and Edgar refused to say where you were. I suppose you've been busy carrying out some private business, perhaps something to do with the festive season."

Glancing over her shoulder, Evie was amazed to see Henrietta talking and writing at the same time.

Henrietta continued, "And Millicent was nowhere to be found, so we all assumed you were both hiding somewhere working on a surprise for us. But then I asked for Edmonds to bring the motor car around and that's when everything fell into place because Edgar said Edmonds was not available. Was I right to think you'd all gone off somewhere?" Henrietta skimmed through what she'd written. Nodding, she smiled and continued writing… and talking.

"Of course, you are well within your rights to... Oh, dear, I lost my train of thought and Gertrude is going to wonder why I think she is well within her rights. She never is because her sense of right is questionable. Perhaps I can make that my gift to her and allow her to believe she has a right to do as she pleases." This time, Henrietta set her fountain pen down and sat back to look at Evie. Looking puzzled, Henrietta studied her before saying, "Something's happened."

Evie's shoulders rose and fell. "I'm afraid so."

Henrietta shifted in her seat and gave Evie her full attention.

Just as Evie was about to break the news, Millicent walked in. She took in the scene and sidled over to a corner where she sat down and opened her notebook.

Evie glanced at the door and, before anyone else could walk in, said, "Millicent and I found a dead body."

"Good heavens, Evangeline. I'm beginning to think you make a habit of finding dead bodies." Reaching for her fountain pen, Henrietta straightened it. "When did this happen?" She picked up the letter she'd been writing and folded the sheath of paper.

"This morning."

Searching through a drawer, Henrietta rifled through the contents. Not finding what she was looking for, she searched through another one. "Don't mind me. I'm looking for an envelope. This morning, did you say?"

"Yes, when we went out."

"How very odd. What were you doing when you found the body?"

Evie didn't wish to go into great detail, so she gave Henrietta a brief explanation.

"You're making garlands for Christmas. How lovely. What was the body doing in the woods?"

"We don't know and, to be perfectly honest, I really don't have any answers. Tom is out there waiting for the police to arrive. I suppose we'll know more when he returns."

"Aha! I found them." Henrietta held an envelope in her hand and waved it. "They are in the same place they have been for as long as I can remember." She uncapped her fountain pen and addressed the envelope. Inserting her letter, she sealed the envelope and stood up. "I must make sure this goes off today. Otherwise, it might not reach Gertrude and that means I'll not hear from her until after Christmas, which would be a great pity because she always gets herself into such a state because the house will be full of people she only ever sees once a year and she can only think about the many reasons why she doesn't like them, never mind that for the rest of the year she will bemoan the fact she only gets to see them once a year."

Henrietta wavered and looked at the desk. "I think I have everything. Yes, I do." Smiling and waving the envelope, almost as if to justify her exodus, Henrietta left the room.

Evie gaped at the door.

"Well, that was odd. At least, I found it odd," Millicent said. "Was it just me or did you find her ladyship's behavior odd?" Millicent looked down at her notebook. "I took the liberty of jotting down a few observations as they occurred to me. Her ladyship did not express any curiosity over the dead person."

Evie nodded. Any other person would have asked about the identity of the dead person and whether or not the death had looked like an accident. Although, most people would simply jump to conclusions and say there was a killer on the loose.

Millicent had made the same observation. As well as others.

"Her ladyship seemed to be more interested in her letter than in what you were saying and she remained calm. How can anyone be calm when they hear about a dead person found in the woods? As for wanting to post the letter, well, she could have asked me. In fact, that's the reason there is a little bell sitting on the writing desk." Millicent turned toward the door. "She only needs to place the envelope on the salver by the front door and a footman will take care of it. She should be back by now. Then again, she might have no intention of returning. But how long can she stay away? It will be luncheon soon and then there's afternoon tea and dinner. She'll have to face you again. Milady, I think you should brace yourself for another night full of tales about their trip to town. I believe her ladyship is doing her best to avoid the subject. Although, I'm not quite sure what that might be. Do you agree, milady?"

Evie had no idea what to say.

At the very least, the Henrietta she knew would have gasped and clutched her throat. Instead, she had distracted herself with her letter. Millicent was right. Henrietta had been trying to avoid the subject.

The door opened and a footman entered and set a tray down on the table.

Thanking him, Evie helped herself to a cup of tea. She savored the first sip and sighed with contentment. "I really needed this." Setting her cup down, she turned to Millicent and encouraged her to have some tea.

"Very well, if you insist, milady. Although, every time I am invited to cross the line, I have to explain myself to everyone downstairs because, of course, word travels faster than the wind in this house."

It took a moment for Evie to understand her meaning. Yes, there were always lines dividing those who lived upstairs and those who worked in the house.

"You're special, Millicent."

Millicent laughed. "If I tell them that, I'll never live it down, and I doubt I'd get away without someone first giving me a clip in the ear."

Making herself comfortable, Evie said, "What I really find odd is that in the last few days I've been asking myself what Henrietta would say and do."

Millicent's eyes widened in surprise. "Why would you do that, milady?"

"Henrietta has very particular ways of dealing with situations and there have been times when I've been rather impressed and wished I could possess some of her wit."

Millicent still looked surprised. "If you ask me, trying to be like her is asking for trouble. It's like wanting to age and…" Millicent lowered her voice to a conspiratorial whisper, "go a bit nutty before your time."

It hadn't occurred to Evie to think of it in those terms. "Have some cake, Millicent." Gesturing to her notebook, she asked, "What else did you write down?"

"I did notice another minute detail. It might be something or it might be nothing. When she turned back to her letter and to writing the address, she uncapped her fountain pen and stilled, almost as if hesitating. Actually, almost as if a thought had come to her and she had to focus on it."

"You did well. I missed that."

Patting her notebook, Millicent said, "It's all here. Would you like me to jot down some notes about this morning while it's still fresh in my mind? Although, I'm not likely to forget any of it. In fact, I'll probably toss and turn all night, even after I look under my bed and in the wardrobe to make sure there isn't someone hiding in there, waiting to kill me."

"Yes, that could be helpful." Evie took a sip of her tea and added, "Yes, taking notes... Mmm. Very helpful. Although, I'm sure it would also help you to check under the bed."

Millicent grinned. "And the wardrobe."

Laughing, they both looked at the clock on the mantle.

Evie knew the police would want to speak with her. A part of her wished they would be satisfied with the information Tom gave them. What more could the police want to know? They had been out and about collecting some holly for garlands and had stumbled upon a dead body.

Setting her tea cup down, Millicent said, "I hope the police don't suspect us."

Evie grumbled. "They won't have any reason to, Millicent."

For once, Millicent chose to remain silent. However, her silence spoke volumes.

We'll see...

Evie finished her tea and stood up to pour herself another cup. "I was rather hoping I could count on Henrietta to spread the word to the others, but I believe she will surprise us all and keep the information to herself." As she took her seat again, the sound of a commotion erupted out in the hall.

Millicent rushed to the door and peered out. Jumping back, she closed the door and mouthed, "It's the Winchester lads. They're looking for you."

Evie heard them hollering her name, the voices coming from different directions.

What sounded like a series of thunderous claps silenced them all.

"Edgar has them under control, milady. I'm sure he'll steer them away from here. I saw him moving toward this door, no doubt to stop them from entering."

Edgar's voice echoed from the hall. "Stop that this instant. What are you doing? Take your hands off me…"

Millicent now had her ear pressed to the door but the shake of her head suggested she hadn't been able to hear anything to explain Edgar's outburst. "I hope they're not trying to tie him up."

They were both startled by a sharp knock on the window pane and Brazen Winchester's face pressed against the glass. Despite the thick glass pane, they heard him call out to the others. "Cousin Evie is in the drawing room."

CHAPTER 6

Tis the season to raise a ruckus

The drawing room

The drawing room door was flung open. Caught by surprise, Millicent jumped back, lost her footing and fell to the floor with a loud whoosh.

The Winchester brothers all piled in. After helping Millicent to her feet, Wilbur turned to Evie, his eyes wild with excitement as he demanded, "Cousin Evie, is it true you found a dead body?"

Edgar stood at the door looking quite distraught. Evie gave him a nod of understanding. There was really nothing more he could have done.

Sighing, Edgar shook his head and retreated.

"How on earth did you find out?" Edmonds had driven them to the house and had then sped away to collect Tom. She knew Millicent hadn't said anything and Edgar's discretion could never be faulted.

Henrietta?

Had she actually rushed off to alert the others?

"So it is true." Brazen huffed out a breath. "Where? When? How?"

Instead of waiting for a response, Brazen and Wilbur Winchester launched into a debate, tossing around ideas and creating a sequence of events, all leading to the discovery of a body. The suggestions were mostly wild products of their imagination, including a man emerging from the woods, a knife stuck in his back, stopping to look to the right and then the left before stepping onto the road and right into the path of the motor car driven by Edmonds. That had been Brazen's suggestion and Wilbur had ridiculed the idea of someone with a knife poking out from his back actually stopping to check for traffic.

Realizing he'd left something out, Brazen turned to Evie and asked, "Who?"

"Would you like me to answer or would you prefer to discuss possible victims with Wilbur?"

Brazen took a moment to consider the options and, to Evie's surprise, he chose to entertain possible candidates with Wilbur.

In the short time they'd been staying at Halton House, they had both become familiar with the villagers and could name them better than Evie ever could.

"Mrs. Constance Lloyd," Wilbur suggested.

Brazen complained, "No, not Connie. She bakes the best pies in the village."

They both turned to Evie, with Brazen asking, "Was it Connie?"

"No."

"Was it a woman?"

"No."

"Are you sure? I'm now thinking it might have been Mrs. Greer."

Wilbur elbowed Brazen. "Just because Mrs. Greer chased you away with a pitchfork and warned you off her daughter doesn't mean you can picture her as the victim." Regardless, Wilbur turned to Evie, "Are you sure it wasn't a woman?"

Evie smiled. "I'm quite confident it wasn't."

Brazen and Wilbur continued with their guessing game, tossing one name after the other. It seemed the brothers had been enjoying quite a few adventures involving the villagers.

After their morning's experience, Evie welcomed the distraction and she could see Millicent was equally captivated, sitting on the edge of her seat, enjoying the spectacle.

"Mr. Wiltmore." Brazen nodded. "It has to be him."

Eugene snorted. Without taking his eyes away from the piece of wood he'd been whittling, he said, "You want it to be him because he didn't like you pointing out that whiskey was spelled wrong on the bottle."

That caught Evie's attention. She hadn't heard any stories about a clash with Mr. Wiltmore. "When did this happen?"

"A couple of weeks ago," Wilbur said. Turning to Eugene, he kicked him. "Quit making a mess."

Picking up the little curls of wood, Eugene stood up and went to stand by the fireplace where he continued his whittling.

Still interested by their encounter with Mr. Wiltmore, Evie asked, "Where?"

"He invited us to his house."

"Why?"

She'd been about to ask the same question, but Millicent beat her to it.

"He needed a piece of furniture moved and he lured us in with a promise of some very fine whiskey," Wilbur explained and added, "Brazen took exception to the fact he brought out a bottle that wasn't whiskey."

Enthralled by the tale, Millicent asked, "What was it?"

Brazen growled. "It was whisky."

"I don't understand."

"It wasn't whiskey. It was whisky."

Wilbur elbowed him. "How is Millicent supposed to know the difference? You're supposed to say whisky with a Scottish brogue."

"I did."

Sensing a squabble in the making, Evie took the temperature of the room. Eugene stood by the fireplace, still whittling. Clarence and Theodore were grumbling about the story because they'd been left out of the adventure, and Nathaniel, the quiet one of the group, sat back with his legs stretched out and crossed at the ankles.

Despite having spent the morning working on their motor cars, all six men were dressed in the height of fashion. If any of them had rolled up their sleeves, they would have tidied up their clothes before coming back inside the house.

Clarence and Theodore escalated their grievances by expressing the injustice of it all and what they deemed to be a selfish act of leaving them out.

Voices were hitched.

Accusations were hurled.

Fists were pumped in the air.

Mesmerized, Evie watched the brothers tease each other. She knew there would a breaking point and hoped it didn't come to that because there were quite a few valuable vases scattered around the drawing room.

When Clarence and Theodore made their move by crossing an invisible line, Nathaniel grinned, almost as if he'd seen it coming. He looked at Eugene, dug inside his pocket, produced a crisp ten pound banknote and pointed at Clarence and Theodore, thereby placing a bet on them. Eugene shrugged and, equalling the amount, placed it on the mantle and resumed his whittling.

"A Macallan whiskey?" Clarence sputtered.

"Yes, what of it?" Brazen challenged.

Clarence growled and Wilbur made the situation worse by saying Brazen had taunted Mr. Wiltmore into opening the bottle because a whiskey with an obvious spelling error on the label couldn't possibly be any good.

"Boys," Nathaniel exploded.

Evie thought he was about to put an end to the argument before it turned into a physical skirmish. Instead, Nathaniel hitched his head and pointed to the door.

"Take it out to the hall. You don't want to break Cousin Evie's nice things."

Before Evie could bring order to the house, the four of them pushed and shoved each other out of the drawing room. Not one to miss out, Millicent rushed out after them.

Evie followed fast on their heels saying, "There are valuables in here too."

Just as they all burst out into the hall, Sarah and Toodles were making their way down the stairs and Henrietta happened to be crossing the hall.

Seeing the Winchester boys removing their coats and rolling up their sleeves, Henrietta clapped and exclaimed, "Oh, goodie. Some excitement."

Edgar appeared and came to an abrupt stop, his arms flapping about as he propelled himself toward them and tried to herd them all back in the drawing room.

"And what's more, he has several bottles," Brazen teased and caught Clarence by surprise. Grabbing him in a stranglehold, he ruffled his hair and demanded that he yield.

"Never!"

"Yield."

"You killed him just to get the bottles. Admit it."

Evie had been trying to remain serious and disapproving, but failed when she burst out laughing.

The timing could not have been worse.

Millicent, who stood next to her, tugged on her sleeve. "Milady!"

When Evie looked at her, Millicent nudged her head toward the front door.

Oh, good heavens.

Tom stood there, looking aghast.

Next to him, a man in a suit pushed his hat back and stared in disbelief, while another man in a constable's uniform blew his whistle.

CHAPTER 7

Talking utter baubles

The library

*D*etective Inspector Everett stood in front of the large mahogany desk, his coat pushed back, his fingers hitched inside his vest pockets. A constable stood next to him, a notebook in hand while another constable stood at attention near the door.

Henrietta looked intrigued, Toodles looked amused, and Sarah looked mystified. Evie didn't blame her.

It had taken both constables to break up the skirmish between Brazen and Clarence who looked somewhat disheveled, although he had done his best to restore order by raking his fingers through his hair.

Tom stood leaning against the fireplace, his arms crossed, his gaze bouncing between one Winchester and the other, as if to ensure they would stay in place and not move a hairsbreadth from where they sat.

Evie knew Edgar was hovering out in the hall, close to the door and, no doubt, he had been joined by some of the footmen.

The detective cleared his throat. "This morning, Lady Woodridge found a dead body in the woods. We will be speaking with each of you separately. At this point, we are collecting information." He swept his gaze across the room, studying everyone present. "I will be conducting the interview in the drawing room and I would like everyone to remain in this room. One of the constables will be present."

While he didn't say it, Evie assumed he wished to make sure everyone would remain under close supervision.

The detective pointed to Brazen. "I'll speak to you first."

"That's odd," Millicent whispered. "Why doesn't he start with us? We're the ones who found the body."

The constable with the notebook followed the detective and Brazen out of the room and everyone shifted, relaxed, and breathed a sigh of relief.

Toodles spoke up first, "Can we have some refreshments, please?"

Evie didn't need to pull the bell cord because Edgar was already at the door letting Toodles know it would be organized.

"Do we know who it is?" Sarah asked.

Evie looked at the constable who appeared to be

looking into space but she suspected was, in fact, keeping a close eye on them and had even been assigned the task of listening to everything said in the room.

Distracted, Evie said, "I didn't see his face." Any other response would have been conjecture.

"Why not?" Henrietta asked. "It seems to me that is the first thing one would do."

"He was face down, Henrietta, and I didn't wish to disturb the scene."

Henrietta sniffed. "Let's hope the detective takes that into account."

Toodles laughed.

Giving her a raised eyebrow look, Henrietta said, "I'm not sure what you find amusing."

"The very idea that the detective would think Birdie might have killed him, but she's not a bad sort because she didn't disturb the scene of the crime."

Unwilling to acknowledge the reasonable explanation, Henrietta lifted her chin. "All I'm saying is that it should count for something." Henrietta turned to Millicent. "Were you present? Yes, of course, and you must have an idea about the person's identity. Could you see any obvious injuries?"

Millicent shook her head. "I didn't get close enough, milady. In fact, when I saw her ladyship feeling for a pulse, I panicked."

"I don't blame you. Ah, here's Edgar with the tea. Very good timing, my dear man. What would we do without you?"

As Henrietta helped herself to a drink, she eyed the Winchester brothers. "I dare say, you'll have some explaining to do. Can you all confirm your whereabouts in the last twenty-four hours? Yes, of course, you were all here." Henrietta then turned to the constable. "Would you care for some tea?"

The constable appeared to want to accept. Instead, he straightened and shook his head.

Henrietta gave him an impish smile. "I hope you don't feel I was testing you."

As everyone helped themselves to tea, Evie stood up and joined Tom by the fireplace. "You haven't said a word since you arrived."

"My apologies, Countess, I got caught up in the moment. Would you mind telling me what they were arguing about?"

"I'm not entirely sure. It started with them feeling they'd missed out on something because they weren't there to find a dead body and it escalated when Brazen talked about..." She broke off and frowned. "I honestly don't know. Sometimes I think they just need to release all that pent up energy they seem to have."

Tom frowned. "Why did Clarence accuse him of killing someone?"

"Ah, yes. The timing was rather unfortunate."

"Incriminating," Tom muttered. "No doubt the detective jumped to all sorts of conclusions. In the past, I've had to clean up after them but this might be too big. Actually, it might be a good lesson for them."

Evie leaned in and whispered, "Is it Mr. Jackson?"

"Yes. One of the constables identified him, and I heard the detective say he must have been struck on the side of the head because he found a serious bruise."

Evie had approached the body from one side so she

assumed the wound had been on the other side of the head.

"You're not shocked or surprised to learn it was Mr. Jackson," Tom said.

"No, I assumed it was him but only because of the severe black clothes he wore. I noticed something about his coat. It seemed to be pulled up, almost as if he'd been dragged by the lapels. He must have been carried there because I didn't see any drag marks. Yes, that makes sense to me. He was carried there and then dragged further in, well out of sight."

Tom lowered his voice. "What were you doing there? Of all the places to be…" Tom broke off and then apologized. "It's bad timing and too much of a coincidence. What with you having that clash with Mr. Jackson."

The detective was bound to find out about that. If he was any good at his job, he would eventually speak with anyone who had been in contact with Mr. Jackson and that would include Mr. Wiltmore and Mrs. Hunter.

Evie closed her eyes and moaned softly.

There were witnesses to her clash with Mr. Jackson.

"What is it?" Tom asked.

"I'm reminding myself to take care when speaking with the detective. I hope he's not the sort to jump to conclusions." Glancing around the room, she noticed the constable watching her. "Perhaps honesty will be the best policy." Evie went on to explain that, instead of waiting to see if the detective rounded up everyone who'd seen Mr. Jackson, she should provide the information herself.

Tom suggested, "Start by expressing dismay at the unfortunate turn of events."

"That will only work if the detective is sensible." When

Tom didn't offer any assurances, Evie nudged him. "Is he?"

"He likes facts. I watched him approach the scene with an eagle eye, scrutinizing the ground every step of the way and then spending a considerable amount of time looking at the body from a safe distance before approaching it. He began by looking at the soles of the shoes and he worked his way up."

That meant he must have noticed the positioning of Mr. Jackson's arms and the state of his clothes.

"Why do you think he chose to interview people in the drawing room?" Out in the hall, the detective had actually asked where the door led to and then he'd asked if there was another large room. Edgar had pointed out the library and the detective had signaled for everyone to go there. The drawing room would have been closer.

"I haven't given it any thought," Tom admitted.

"It seems strange. If given a choice, men would always veer toward a library than a drawing room." Evie studied the wood paneling and dark colored furniture. "Libraries look more masculine and... serious. Whereas drawing rooms are more frivolous."

Tom looked at her with curiosity. "Is your mind wandering or are you just making lighthearted conversation?"

Instead of answering, she said, "The drawing room would be more disarming. Yes, people relax in drawing rooms. The walls are light colored and the furniture colorful. The windows allow all that bright light in. Whereas here, the thick curtains are half drawn, all the furniture is dark and the wood paneling gives the room a general air of seriousness." Evie nodded. "He's employing stealth tactics."

The constable who had accompanied the detective appeared at the door and he asked Clarence to accompany him.

"The troublemakers are being rounded up," Tom mused. "He's prioritizing."

"Is the detective working the case by himself?"

"No, there's another one. Detective Constable Jenkins. He stayed behind to wait for the body to be taken away."

"And what's he like?"

"He whistles."

"What's that supposed to mean?"

Tom shrugged. "It could mean anything. Whistling might be a cover for a devious mind. Or he might be a happy-go-lucky fellow who takes everything in his stride. Or maybe he enjoys working crime scenes."

Henrietta drew everyone's attention by asking, "Where's Brazen? You don't suppose he's been taken into custody. And how much longer is this going to take?" She turned to the constable. "At this rate, I'll be offering you lunch."

Evie whispered, "Henrietta has been acting strangely."

"How so?"

"She's been evasive. When I told her about discovering the body, she didn't ask any questions. She'd been writing a letter and she continued to do so as I spoke. When she finished, she rushed off."

Once again, Henrietta spoke up and captured everyone's attention. "I've just realized there might be a killer in this room."

Brazen walked in and walked straight to the table where he poured himself a cup of tea.

"Oh, here he is. We thought you'd been hauled away to prison."

Toodles snorted. "I believe you were the only one to say that."

Ignoring her remark, Henrietta looked at Brazen and asked, "Are you under suspicion?"

"I will be if Mr. Wiltmore turns up dead."

"Mr. Wiltmore, the solicitor? Why would you kill… I mean, why would anyone kill him?"

Sarah interrupted by saying, "I think he's retired now, Henrietta."

"Is that any reason to kill him?"

"No one's killed him, Henrietta."

Henrietta nudged her head toward Brazen. "Not yet."

Everyone turned to the constable to see his reaction to Henrietta's outburst.

Noticing this, Henrietta laughed. "Oh, don't mind me. I'm just getting into the spirit of things."

The constable blinked but did not otherwise respond.

Brazen took a sip of his tea and, walking about the room, said, "I've been put on notice. Now I'm not sure what I'll do about that. Should I remain in the house or should I make sure nothing happens to Mr. Wiltmore?" He stopped in front of the constable. "You didn't hear that."

Henrietta laughed. "I'm sure he did, Brazen. But there's an idea, we should confuse the constable by acting suspicious."

Clarence walked in and headed straight to the window where he stood with his hands thrust inside his pockets.

"The detective seems to think I'm a troublemaker and he'll be keeping a close eye on me." He turned and looked at Brazen. "And you. We could have fun with this."

Oh, dear heavens...

Evie turned to Tom. "You'll have your hands full reining them in."

"Where did I leave my whip?" Tom muttered.

"Lady Woodridge, the detective is ready for you now."

Henrietta chirped, "He used Brazen and Clarence to warm up. Evangeline, don't let your guard down."

CHAPTER 8

Lady Woodridge incriminates herself

The drawing room

"Lady Woodridge, please take a seat."

Evie wanted to say she preferred to stand for no other reason than to defy him. In her mind, this interview was entirely unnecessary and a waste of police resources and time.

As she sat down, Evie found herself smiling because she realized she'd just sounded like Henrietta.

The day before, she had wondered what Henrietta would do and say if she had to meet Mr. Jackson whose reputation had preceded him. Now she had to wonder if she was aspiring to greater wisdom or to becoming more eccentric.

The detective surprised Evie by asking, "And how is the mood in the library?"

"Lively and, despite the circumstances, quite entertaining. The scene you encountered when you arrived was somewhat unusual. We have become accustomed to the boys' antics, but I imagine a stranger would be mystified by it all."

"The boys? They are grown men."

"Indeed, but they behave like rambunctious boys. They recently acquired a couple of run down motor cars, which have kept them busy and out of mischief but, like boys with toys, they are easily distracted." Evie knew she'd provided more information than had been required or even expected, but she rather enjoyed taking charge of the moment. Again, she smiled and thought Henrietta would be proud of her.

"They are very protective of you."

Evie smiled. "I would never call to question their loyalty or chivalry. However, I suspect they are influenced by their surroundings."

It took a moment for the detective to make the connection. "The armors and swords and whatnot on display in the hall."

"Yes, not to mention the pistols and longbows and arrows."

"Mr. Winchester said you'd been gathering holly. You make your own garlands?"

"Doesn't everyone?" Evie wasn't at all surprised by the swift change of subject. If she'd been interviewed in the library, she might have been sitting on the edge of her seat. The drawing room offered a more inviting and relaxed setting. As if that wasn't enough, he had employed the tactic of disarming her with small talk.

"My wife usually takes care of all those things. I suppose she does make her own."

"You might want to find out and perhaps compliment her," Evie suggested.

Nodding, he asked, "Were you surprised to find Mr. Jackson's body in the woods?"

Evie wasted no time in saying, "I was actually surprised to find a body in the woods."

"Did you immediately know it was Mr. Jackson?"

"I had my suspicion, but I didn't care to confirm it because it involved turning the body over."

"How did you know he was dead?"

"I couldn't see him breathing. I'm no expert on the matter. For all I knew, he might have been a shallow breather. So I actually felt for a pulse. His body was cold."

"And then what did you do?"

"I sent my lady's maid to get help. Edmonds, the chauffeur, had been waiting by the side of the road, so Millicent didn't have far to go. He then drove back to the house to alert Mr. Winchester."

"And what did you do while you waited?"

"I stood still and I looked around me. I think I was trying to avoid looking at the body. I can't say with any certainty, but I believe I might have been in shock and denial."

"Did you know Mr. Jackson well?"

"I'd met him yesterday for the first time." Evie sensed alarm bells ringing. She needed to proceed with caution because the detective had already shown himself to be quite capable of catching her by surprise.

"What did you think of him?"

She hadn't expected that question. "I didn't care for his manner."

"What was wrong with his manner?" He smiled. "Was he not reverential enough?"

"What?"

"Some people enjoy receiving a certain degree of respect, with smiles and flattery and blandishments. While others prefer to be treated like everyone else. Equally."

Evie knew he was referring to class distinction, but she refused to take the bait. "After that first encounter, I walked away believing Mr. Jackson would treat everyone in the same manner."

"Is that good or bad?"

"He was abrupt and some people equate that with being rude."

"Did you leave on good terms?"

Evie resisted the urge to shift in her seat and make herself more comfortable. "When I left, I felt disappointed. While I hadn't formed any firm opinions about him, I'd hoped he would be a pleasant man to deal with. Actually, I found myself excusing his behavior."

"How so?"

"I prefer to be open-minded and make allowances. Everyone has bad days. He'd been dressed in severe black, so I thought he might have had a recent loss in his life."

"That's very considerate of you."

"I like to think of myself as fair-minded. However,

given time and different circumstances, I believe his manner would have remained unchanged."

"Did you let the Winchester brothers know about your experience with Mr. Jackson?"

"No, I didn't see any reason to share something which needed to be resolved."

"Resolved? In what way?"

Evie regretted her choice of words. She had done well to steer him away from the subject of Mr Jackson's rudeness, only to then draw him back. "Mr. Jackson had recently taken up his position as headmaster and I am on the board so we were going to liaise on a regular basis. We needed to get our priorities straightened. He was here to do a job and I'd hoped his abrupt manner didn't get in the way."

"You sound very passionate about the subject."

"Detective, Mr. Jackson was in charge of the village children."

"And if his manner hadn't improved? What would you have done?"

"I would have recommended a swift dismissal."

"Wouldn't you worry about him moving somewhere else and subjecting others to his abrupt manner?"

She had walked right into a trap. A trap entirely of her own making. "Detective, I met the man yesterday. Then I returned to Halton House and got on with my day. This morning, I set off with my lady's maid in search of some holly and found a body. I had no time to plot the man's demise."

"Perhaps someone did you a favor." The detective turned and had a word with the constable who'd been taking notes.

Evie only then became aware of his presence. She watched as the constable searched for something in his notebook and pointed at a page.

The detective straightened and said, "Remind me again, did the Winchester brothers know about your clash with Mr. Jackson?"

"Clash?"

"My apologies. I thought you said you'd had a clash with Mr. Jackson."

She had said no such thing. At least, she didn't think she had.

Evie knew the detective was waiting for a response. However, the question had caught her by surprise and she knew her honest answer would reflect badly on the Winchesters.

Had Brazen or Clarence mentioned hearing the news about her encounter with Mr. Jackson?

Good heavens. Had either of them bragged about wanting to teach Mr. Jackson a lesson?

"News about my disagreement had reached the house," she finally admitted.

"It must have been a significant disagreement. How do you think news traveled so fast?"

"I couldn't really say, detective."

"Did someone actually witness it?"

"Witness what, detective?"

"The disagreement."

Evie nodded. "There were two others present at the meeting. Mrs. Hunter and Mr. Wiltmore. They are both members of the board."

Both Evie and the detective looked at the constable who wrote the names and underlined them.

"Did you say your lady's maid accompanied you?"

"Yes."

"Was she present at the meeting?"

Oh, dear...

"Yes, she was. Millicent is also my private secretary. She was there to take notes."

Oh, dear...

Evie scolded herself for giving him too much information.

"Well then, I think we should speak with Millicent. Thank you, Lady Woodridge."

CHAPTER 9

Lady Woodridge simmers and fumes

The library

When Evie returned to the library, she walked straight toward the window and was soon joined by Tom.

"Countess?"

She spoke through gritted teeth. "Not now, Tom. I'm fuming."

Everyone had watched her entrance, their eyes bright with curiosity. Now, they were all murmuring, no doubt offering their opinions on why she was fuming.

The constable appeared at the door and asked for Millicent.

The room fell silent and everyone turned to look at Evie's secretary and lady's maid.

"What? Me? Why?" Millicent looked about the room as if searching for someone to back her up and bail her out.

"The detective is speaking with everyone, miss."

"But I'm a nobody. What does he think I know? I really don't know anything. Most of the time, I don't know my left foot from my right."

"Miss, he's waiting."

"Oh, very well." Millicent rose to her feet and straightened her clothes. "But I don't see what I can possibly say that will matter one way or the other."

Brazen winked at Millicent. "Don't worry, darlin'. If they haul you off to jail, we'll break you out."

Evie shook her head. "I think we should have a glass of sherry waiting for Millicent." Turning, she looked at the clock. "We're going to have a late luncheon, although I don't see why we should be inconvenienced." While she knew they were in the process of assisting with an investigation, she couldn't help feeling as she did because she knew no one here was responsible for Mr. Jackson's death. Catching Edgar's attention, she said, "Please let everyone downstairs know they should go ahead and have luncheon."

"Countess, you could ask the detective to leave and return at a more convenient time. This is your domain."

True.

Could she pull rank? And risk coming across as uncooperative? What would that say about her?

She signaled to Brazen and Wilbur and asked, "Have they said anything?"

"No, and that worries me. It usually means they're

plotting. I'll have to set a curfew, from midnight to midnight. No one leaves the house."

"That's rather extreme. That means they'll be underfoot all day long."

Tom glared at his cousins. "I hadn't thought of that. It's a high price to pay but we'll have to grin and bear it. I can't have them going around killing people."

"Tom!"

He smiled at Evie. "Feeling better?"

"Oh, I see. You were trying to cheer me up."

"Yes, I was, however, I'm serious about the curfew. You haven't seen them at their worst."

"Heavens. What else can they possibly get up?"

"You really don't want to know, Countess." Tom glanced over his shoulder and then murmured, "Have you noticed anything odd about Henrietta? Anything unusually odd?" Giving her a brisk smile, he added, "Anything extraordinarily odd?"

"I think I know what you mean, Tom. Even odder than usual."

"Yes, that's it."

"I am inclined to say yes. However, it is the silly season and Henrietta gets very excited. There's so much happening, with everyone running around trying to tie up loose ends before the end of the year and planning for the festive season."

Henrietta, Sarah, and Toodles had moved to a small table and were playing a game of cards. The Winchesters were craning their necks and Brazen was hovering around, either watching the card game or itching to join in.

Evie noticed Henrietta casting furtive glances around.

This was unusual for her. Henrietta preferred the direct approach and never tried to hide her intentions. If she wanted to say something, she always drew everyone's attention, making sure she was in full command of the podium.

"Millicent believes Henrietta is hiding something. I can't imagine what that might be." Evie tried to remember if she'd already mentioned this. "I can't believe the way this day has turned out. My mind is a whirlpool."

Tom agreed. "There's never a warning shot."

"I wonder about that." After her unfortunate encounter with Mr. Jackson, she should have expected something horrible to happen. "I still can't believe he's dead."

He wasn't just dead, Evie thought.

Mr. Jackson had been killed and that made him a murder victim.

Tom smiled at her. "I believe you are about to propose something."

"I'm sure I don't know what you mean. Although, I wouldn't mind knowing if he had any enemies." Evie frowned. Someone killed him and then tried to hide his body.

"He was relatively new to the village. Too new to have made enemies," Tom said.

"That's a good point. We don't really know anything about him except that he is new to the village." At the first opportunity, she'd like to have a word with Mrs. Hunter and Mr. Wiltmore.

Evie continued, "I mentioned the two board members present at yesterday's meeting. I'm sure the police will want to speak with them. I suppose I'll have to get in line. They interviewed Mr. Jackson for the position and would have seen his credentials." Evie drew in a deep breath. Mrs. Hunter and Mr. Wiltmore had both cowered in Mr. Jackson's presence. She had no trouble picturing him bullying them into giving him the position.

"What sort of background check would they have done?" Tom asked.

"Other than to read the letters of reference? None. I can't imagine them delving into his background or asking any questions that would have revealed anything significant about him."

Millicent returned and headed straight for a chair. Settling down, she uncapped her fountain pen and began writing in her notebook.

The constable stood at the door and pointed to Theodore Winchester.

"Are you ready to talk about it?" Tom asked.

Evie knew exactly what he was referring to. "Detective Inspector Everett is cunning and, I'm afraid, he got the better of me."

"I see."

"I'm not sure that you do."

"Did he trick you into saying something you would have preferred to keep to yourself?" Tom asked.

"It all depends on how he interprets what I said." Evie didn't have to guess where his mind had been headed. Why would he focus on the Winchesters? "He's very good at putting people on edge and then engaging them in light conversation."

"And waiting like a snake to strike?" Tom asked.

"Precisely."

Detective Inspector Everett walked in and thanked everyone for their time.

Evie looked at Henrietta. She was shuffling the cards and didn't even look up. Toodles and Sarah were waiting for Henrietta to deal the hand and both kept their gazes fixed on the cards. To Evie, it looked as if they had all lost interest in the investigation and were waiting for it to be over so they could get on with their day.

She didn't blame them.

Tom stepped forward. "Detective, I'll walk you out."

"Try to get information out of him," Evie whispered.

Everyone stirred, including Henrietta.

Brazen spoke up first, "Well, that was an interesting turn of events. Where do we start?"

Wilbur's shoulder connected with Brazen's shoulder. "You want to get us all into trouble?"

"Yes."

Wilbur grinned and turned to Evie. "It would be interesting to see if we can find the killer first."

Oh, dear heavens.

"I know you are well intentioned, but I feel it would be best if we all let the police handle the matter. And considering what we've all just been through, I would advise you all to stay right here and not go wandering off."

"Of course, Cousin Evie. Whatever you say. Although, I'm sure you're just saying that because you don't wish us to get into trouble."

Millicent stood up and approached Evie. "He was a beast."

"Detective Inspector Everett?"

"He cornered me. I had my back to the wall."

"What?"

"One moment, he was asking me if I could recommend a good place for a hot meal and, suddenly, he cracked the whip and lashed out with a question I hadn't expected."

"Millicent, when you say you had your back to the wall, you don't mean that literally… Do you?"

"Oh, no. I was sitting down." Millicent grinned. "Actually, I took my time settling down. First I complained about the light hitting my eye and then I complained about being too close to the fireplace, and feeling suddenly hot. So I started fanning myself and huffing and puffing. And that seemed to make him uncomfortable, so I huffed and puffed some more, and asked for some water. I've never seen anyone move so quickly. He rushed out of the drawing room. When he returned, he entered with caution. I think he might have been afraid he'd find me hanging from the chandelier." Millicent's cheeks reddened. "He was really sneaky. Like I said, he pretended to be friendly and then shot out questions that I knew were meant to disarm me."

"I had a similar experience, Millicent. However, you were far more creative than I could ever be. I wished I'd thought of making him uncomfortable."

"I knew I was taking a risk. He could quite easily have sent me to the madhouse." Millicent nodded and looked around the room. "Mr. Winchester is taking his time."

"I asked him to find out all he could. With any luck, he'll return with a full report and we can just get on with our lives." Evie looked out the window. "That sounded odd. After all, someone killed Mr. Jackson. There is a killer in our midst."

"And he might strike again," Millicent mused. "It can't

have been anyone from the village and that's a problem because I don't recall hearing of any strangers coming here."

Had Mr. Jackson pushed someone too far?

"Millicent, you should go and have something to eat."

"What are you going to do, milady?"

Evie knew what she'd like to do. However, putting this nasty business behind her wouldn't sit well with her. She knew she wouldn't last an hour, if that, before asking Tom what he thought about the case or commenting on something the police had done or hadn't done.

"We still have a Christmas pageant to organize. In fact, we'll have to roll up our sleeves, step in, and do whatever Mr. Jackson was going to do."

Millicent smiled. "Only better?"

"Yes."

"We could do the the story you mentioned, The Wind in the Willows Christmas with Mole and Rat and Toad."

"Funny you should mention that. We'll have to go speak with Mrs. Hunter and Mr. Wiltmore." And, in the process, they could prod them for information.

CHAPTER 10

Order in the house!

Luncheon

*E*vie stood outside the dining room and took a moment to collect her thoughts.

Tom had spent a great deal of time talking with Detective Inspector Everett. On the bright side, the detective had been prepared to give him his time, instead of sending him off to mind his own business and take care that none of his wayward cousins got into more trouble than they were probably already in.

When he'd finished talking with the detective, Tom had rounded up his cousins and had marched them off to the yard where he'd given them a good talking to.

According to Millicent, who'd been downstairs in the kitchen, Tom had cracked his whip more than once.

Evie leaned in and pressed her ear to the dining room door. If a pin had dropped, she would have heard it. Had everyone forgotten about luncheon?

She eased the door open and peered inside.

Tom was walking around the table. He stopped next to Brazen, scribbled something on a piece of paper and gave it to him.

He then scribbled something else and gave that piece of paper to Nathaniel. He continued to do this until all his cousins had a piece of paper.

Eugene read his note and snorted.

Clarence leaned back and grunted.

Wilbur and Brazen exchanged papers.

While Theodore and Nathaniel both studied their notes and looked up in thought.

Thinking Tom had set up some sort of game to distract everyone, Evie walked in. As she headed for her place at the table, she realized Henrietta, Sarah, and Toodles hadn't been issued any notes.

Edgar drew the chair out for her. Thanking him, Evie glanced around the table and tried to gage the mood.

She didn't feel any tension and the Winchester brothers didn't seem to be kicking up a fuss.

Evie looked across the table at Tom but he had his eyes down on his plate.

Henrietta leaned in and whispered to Toodles, "Did you get one?"

"One what?"

"A note. I didn't get one." Looking at Tom, Henrietta asked, "Why didn't I get a note?"

"Do you need one?" he asked.

Looking confused, Henrietta said, "I don't know. Do I?"

Wilbur cleared his throat. "My, my, despite the cold, the weather has been rather splendid lately."

Brazen held up his piece of paper, "To which I reply, yes."

Wilbur jabbed his elbow against Brazen's ribs. "You're not supposed to read the instructions."

Clarence snorted. "I saw a flock of birds today. Don't ask what kind of birds they were." He shot Tom a dark look. "I know nothing about birds."

As the others made their brief statements, Tom looked quite pleased with himself.

"We have robins here. They sing in the morning," Sarah said. "But I don't think they fly in flocks."

Evie was puzzled by the fact Henrietta and the others were quite content to talk about birds. Didn't anyone wish to discuss Mr. Jackson's death?

She looked across the table at Tom and considered asking him to share what the detective had told him. He had clearly said something. Otherwise, what could they have talked about all that time?

Tom cleared his throat but he didn't speak. Instead, he gave Theodore a pointed look.

"Oh, right…" Theodore dug inside his coat pocket, drew out the note, and said in a dull monotone, "It's a pity we're too late for the hunt. I would so very much have liked to participate."

"How very odd," Henrietta mused.

Evie looked from one Winchester to the other. Had Tom brought them to heel by demanding that they stick to a script? They had now fallen silent and weren't even taunting each other the way they usually did.

Even Henrietta, Sarah, and Toodles were unusually quiet.

Evie looked down at her plate and realized she'd already eaten half her food without even noticing. Taking a sip of wine, she looked around the table. Since the Winchester brothers had delivered their scripted remarks, no one else had spoken. Evie decided to test the waters.

"The detective must be building a case against someone," Evie said.

The Winchester brothers all looked up and straight at Tom, while Henrietta and the others all reached for their glasses.

"Tom," Evie prompted.

"Yes?"

"Did you hear me?"

"I'm sorry, I must have been lost in my thoughts. This beef is absolutely delicious."

Nathaniel cleared his throat and appeared to be about to say something. His gaze slid toward Tom who looked right back at him, but only for the briefest moment.

If Evie didn't know better, she'd think Tom had just issued a warning.

"Did you want to say something, Nathaniel?" Evie asked.

"Who? Me?" Nathaniel shook his head.

"Are you sure?"

Nathaniel nodded.

Evie studied one brother after the next and then made her selection. Looking at Clarence, she asked, "How is your meal?"

Out of the corner of her eye, Evie saw Tom lower his knife and fork. She glanced back at Clarence and quickly shifted her gaze back to Tom. He was now scowling at Clarence. Was he issuing another warning?

Clarence grinned. "Birds make the most delicious meals."

Straightening and leaning slightly forward, Evie looked at Clarence's plate. He was eating pheasant.

"Wilbur."

"Yes, Ma'am."

"How is your meal?"

"As fine as the weather, which, despite the cold, has been rather splendid lately."

She had her proof. Evie sat back. Unless she was imagining it, Clarence talked about birds and Wilbur mentioned the weather, not once but twice. Tom had given each one of his cousins a topic of conversation to veer away from at their own peril.

"Henrietta!" Evie exclaimed.

Startled, Henrietta looked up, her eyes wide. "Yes, Evangeline?"

Evie plucked the first thought that came to mind. "Do you think we should meddle in the police investigation?"

"Only if you doubt the detective's abilities. Do you?"

"I'm not sure I like him. In fact, I don't like him. If he had interviewed you, I think you would have found him irritating."

"In that case, I'm glad I wasn't subjected to his questions." Henrietta turned to Sarah, "Would you be a dear and pass the salt, please. The beef is prepared to perfection but there are days when I feel the need for more salt."

Eugene smiled. "Once upon a time, salt was used as currency."

Everyone stared at Eugene and waited for him to follow the remark with an explanation.

Eugene added, "The word salary comes from the Latin word sal, for salt. When someone is lousy at their job, he's not worth his salt."

Evie turned to Nathaniel. He was the only one who hadn't made any remarks. "And how is your meal, Nathaniel?"

"It melts in my mouth… like butter. Yes, butter, which is churned until… it becomes butter."

"Fascinating," Henrietta mused.

Grinning, Nathaniel said, "Not as interesting as a Norwegian king demanding a bucket of butter as tax annually."

Why would Tom set boundaries and restrict his cousins to only talking about certain subjects?

He had avoided commenting on her remark about the detective building a case.

Had the detective placed an embargo on the subject?

How ludicrous.

The main course plates were removed and a footman served fruit and cheese. Evie declined and, taking a sip of water, excused herself without any further efforts to engage anyone in conversation.

Stepping out of the dining room, she breathed a sigh of relief, only then realizing how stressful it had been to sit through a meal and put so much effort into having a simple conversation.

She'd never had to work so hard.

"Countess."

Tom had followed her out?

Turning, she saw Tom hurrying after her. "What was that all about?"

Tom rolled his eyes. "My apologies, I should have warned you but, what with one thing or another, I didn't have the opportunity."

"Let me guess. You spoke with the detective and he warned you to discipline your cousins and keep them under a tight leash."

He grinned. "I could not have put it better. We were out in the open, otherwise, I'd suspect you of eavesdropping on the conversation."

"Did he give a reason?"

"More or less. He will not tolerate any interference." Tom looked heavenward. "From anyone."

"Meaning me and you?"

"Mostly you."

Evie gaped at him. "What was your response to that?"

"I told him he was making a grave mistake because your input would be crucial to solving the case." Finding his humor, he added, "Did I do well?"

Evie struck up a pensive pose. "Yes, you went some way toward redeeming yourself. I do have another question. The notes…"

"A stroke of genius, if I do say so myself. I knew asking them to shut up and not discuss the case would be impossible, so I gave them leeway to speak at length, but only on a specific subject."

"And they agreed?"

Smiling, he nodded. "Pretending to argue yesterday morning worked a treat. I'm still holding that over them.

So, for the sake of our matrimonial bliss, they agreed to behave."

"How long for?"

"Until the case is solved."

"Tom! Are you saying we'll be hearing Wilbur drone on about the weather, while Clarence talks about birds and Theodore is limited to discussing the hunt…" Evie stopped and tried to remember the limited subjects the others had tackled.

Tom filled in the rest, "Eugene seems to know a lot about salt and Nathaniel surprised me with information about butter."

"What about Brazen? I can't believe you would hobble him by allowing him to only say yes or no."

"Why not?"

"Tom! That's harsh. Brazen is the chattiest of them all."

"And your point is? He was the one giving me the most grief."

"And how exactly is any of that going to help? At the first opportunity, they will take off and snoop around to their hearts' content."

"No, they won't. If they do, I'll send them back."

"Back where?"

"Back home and they'll be banned from ever setting foot in Halton House."

"Very well. I suppose you know what's best." She looked over his shoulder. "Are we supposed to have another make believe row?"

"No, that's fine. I told them I was coming out to apologize to you."

"That was very gallant of you. Anyhow, I need to organize myself and Millicent. With Mr. Jackson gone, we'll have to meet with the other board members and discuss what we'll do about the Christmas pageant."

"You're going back to the village? Is that wise? Are you going to leave me out of the investigation?"

"What investigation? I have no intention of sticking my nose where it doesn't belong." Evie shrugged. "Not deliberately. As for leaving you, well... You have to stay behind and supervise your wayward relatives." Waving, she swung away and made her way up the stairs.

Tom called out, "Countess, be careful."

CHAPTER 11

The game is afoot

The village

As they approached the place where they had stopped the day before, Evie looked away and into the distance. Despite her efforts, the scene took shape in her mind.

Shuddering, Evie tried to distract herself by asking, "What was the mood like downstairs?"

Millicent shrugged. "The same as ever. Chatty. Everyone had heard about the Winchester skirmish so I had to provide all the details. I don't know what we'll do when they leave."

"I'm sure we'll manage."

Millicent worried her bottom lip. "I'll be sorry to see them go, but they don't appear to be in any hurry to leave."

"I'm just glad they didn't insist on a third wedding ceremony."

Millicent pointed ahead. "Mrs. Hunter lives just off the village green and Mr. Wiltmore lives three houses down from the church. Where would you like to go first?"

This was going to be a surprise, impromptu visit to discuss what to do about the Christmas pageant and how they would deal with Mr. Jackson's demise. Evie assumed both board members had heard about it. She hoped they had because she'd hate to be the bearer of bad news.

"Milady?"

"Mmm?"

"Would you like to go see Mrs. Hunter or Mr. Wiltmore first?"

"Neither one." Evie's eyes widened. "Did I just say that?"

"Yes, you did. At least, I'm sure I heard you. Then again... No, I'm sure I heard you say neither one. Truth be known, I agree. They both showed their true colors. That makes me wonder how Mr. Jackson ever got them to squirm with fear. You stood up to him. I suppose that's because you have a strong character and know how to stand your ground. Some people would say you're stubborn. Those who know you would say you are quite sensitive to bullish behavior and won't stand for it. Anyone could see the board members had been bullied into compliance by Mr. Jackson. Oh... Something just occurred to me. You don't suppose one of them killed him? I mean, just because they appeared to cower in his presence doesn't mean they don't have a breaking point. You can push someone only so far before they actually take matters into their own hands."

Evie tried her best to digest everything Millicent had just said. "I should never have said I don't want to visit either one. However, you're absolutely right about Mrs. Hunter and Mr. Wiltmore. I've never known them to be so compliant and I've never before attended a meeting that was so one-sided. There has always been an easy exchange of ideas and, even when we don't agree, we always find a common ground and compromise."

"And then Mr. Jackson came along," Millicent said. "I wonder what he said to them."

Collecting her thoughts, Evie added, "Actually, I'm more concerned about them not knowing Mr. Jackson has died and having to break the news to them. Also, Mr. Winchester has been charged with the task of keeping his cousins under control. The detective doesn't want them delving into the case. While Mr. Winchester didn't explicitly say that included us, I'm sure it did. I just don't wish to find myself in a situation where I'll feel compelled to ask questions."

"Oh, I thought that was the whole point to this visit."

"Whatever gave you that idea, Millicent?"

Millicent brought out her notebook and skimmed through the pages. "I must have written something down. Here it is." She read through the page and hummed. "I can't really tell if I wrote down something you said or if I scribbled my interpretation of what you said."

"Millicent, what did you write?"

"The game is afoot."

Evie frowned and searched her mind. Had she said

something to suggest to Millicent that they would be asking people questions?

No, she was sure she hadn't.

In fact...

Her focus had been on the Christmas pageant.

Glancing at Millicent, she refrained from correcting her. Perhaps Millicent had read between the lines and jumped to conclusions.

Evie decided to play it safe. "We should prioritize the pageant."

Millicent didn't bother hiding her disappointment.

"However..."

"Yes?"

"We should keep our eyes open."

"And observe?" Millicent nodded. "I'll make sure to take note of everything they say. You never know, they might give themselves away."

Evie recalled every other encounter she'd had with Mrs. Hunter and Mr. Wiltmore. They'd been friendly and easy to engage in conversation. Mrs. Hunter, in particular, had a keen interest in ensuring the local children received all the advantages they could get and, indeed, she believed they were in a position to assist any of the children who showed promise and even those who didn't necessarily excel at anything.

Smiling, Evie remembered Mrs. Hunter saying it was their duty to inspire and had then singled out one of the children saying he would eventually take over his father's farm and spend the rest of his life working the land, but that shouldn't limit him.

"Think how much richer his life will be if we introduce him to great art and literature," Evie whispered.

Millicent hurried to write something down. Thinking she had been inspired, Evie asked her about it.

Millicent's cheeks colored.

"Millicent?" Evie prompted.

"I was just wondering about Mr. Jackson. The detective is going to want to talk to the last person who saw him alive. It can't be us. Remember, we were on our way to have lunch but we found him at the tearoom and beat a hasty retreat."

The motor car slowed down and made a turn. Evie looked around and realized they'd arrived at the village.

They could trace Mr. Jackson's whereabouts right up to the moment they'd seen him at the tearoom. Then, they'd found his body the next morning.

What had happened in-between?

Evie wondered if he'd said anything to Mrs. Hunter and Mr. Wiltmore. They had followed him out of the meeting. Had they spoken with him? Or had they gone their separate ways?

Millicent had been paying attention so she directed Edmonds. "It's the second house on the left."

Edmonds stopped right in front of the house and pushed back his cap.

"We might be a while, Edmonds." The village had already set up a Nativity scene at the church. Evie thought it would be more fun to perform something different for the pageant, and that would require further discussions and planning.

The stone cottage had a large window and two smaller ones facing the street. The front door was painted a light shade of green and had a brass door knocker and a festive wreath. As the cold weather had settled in, there were no colorful plants to brighten the place, however, Evie had driven past the house many times and had noticed a display of pretty blooms with many cottage garden favorites.

"She must know," Millicent murmured. "This is the heart of the village and everyone steps out at least once a day, even in cold weather. You might be spared the dreadful ordeal of having to break the news, milady. Then again, It's possible she doesn't know. We discovered the body and Mr. Winchester alerted the police. All this happened outside the village."

Collecting her handbag, Evie nodded. "There is only one way to find out."

As they made their way to the front door, Millicent said, "She is definitely home. There's smoke billowing from her chimney and Pumpkin is not at the window."

"Pumpkin?"

"Mrs. Hunter's cat."

"I didn't realize you were on friendly terms with Mrs. Hunter."

"I'm not."

"So how do you know her cat's name?"

"Not long ago, I was posting a letter for you and Mrs. Hunter was ahead of me and the postmistress was having one of her chatty days so Mrs. Hunter cut her off by saying she needed to hurry home or expect to find Pumpkin twitching her whiskers in disapproval because she'd promised she would be back in no time."

Evie was about to knock on the door when it opened and Mrs. Hunter stepped out. She was looking down at the ground. When she closed the door behind her, she looked up and reacted by pressing her hand to her throat and gaping at them.

Taking a deep swallow, Mrs. Hunter said, "Lady Woodridge. I was just on my way out."

Evie noticed she hadn't buttoned her coat properly and she hadn't put on a hat.

Mrs. Hunter added, "I was just on my way to post a letter."

Knowing she couldn't ask her to postpone her outing, Evie decided she would at least mention Mr. Jackson's death. "It's dreadful news about Mr. Jackson."

Mrs. Hunter looked at Evie. It must have taken her a full minute to blink. "Mr. Jackson? Has something happened?"

Evie chose her words with great care. As she was about to speak, Millicent said, "He's dead. Someone killed him."

"Oh, dear." Mrs. Hunter pressed her hands to her cheeks. "Oh, dear." Reaching behind her, she opened the door and stumbled inside.

"Mrs. Hunter!" Millicent propelled herself forward and snatched at whatever she could grab, managing to take hold of Mrs. Hunters hand and coat sleeve.

As Millicent helped to steady Mrs. Hunter, Evie had the strangest thought. She heard Nathaniel's voice in her head saying butter wouldn't melt in her mouth.

Butter?

It took a moment to remember that had been Nathaniel's key word.

But why would the phrase come to her, right at that moment?

Hurrying to help Millicent, they both assisted Mrs.

Hunter inside and settled her in a chair by the fireplace. Pumpkin, an orange tabby, looked up from her comfortable bed by the fireplace and yawned. After studying the situation, she stretched and pranced over to Mrs. Hunter.

"Dead?" Mrs Hunter whispered.

"Yes," Millicent hurried to confirm. "Her ladyship and I found him this morning." Her arm shot out and she pointed in the general direction of the woods. "We followed a well-trodden path to get to the holly and, as we were chatting and cutting, her ladyship stumbled and fell on top of him. Can you believe that?"

Mrs. Hunter's eyes widened. "Dead?" She looked at Evie and then back at Millicent. "But we all saw him yesterday."

Millicent gave a stiff nod. "Yes, yesterday he was alive and today he is dead."

"How? Had he been ill?"

Millicent looked at Evie. What could she say? They didn't have a cause of death. Tom had mentioned a blow to the head but Evie knew the police needed to wait for a full report.

"Let me help you out of that coat," Millicent offered. "Would you like a cup of tea? Will that help?"

Mrs. Hunter swallowed and, instead of nodding, she gestured to a small table in the corner of the drawing room.

"Would a glass of sherry help?" Millicent asked.

"Brandy, please."

Millicent hid her surprise by swinging away and rushing toward the small table to pour her a glass. While Millicent didn't express her disapproval of relying on an alcoholic beverage instead of an old-fashioned cup of tea,

Evie could read it all in her face as she returned and handed the glass to Mrs. Hunter.

Millicent's eyebrows hitched up as Mrs. Hunter studied the moderate amount of brandy. With a small shrug, she gulped it down and held out the glass.

"More?" Millicent asked, her tone filled with disbelief.

"Yes, please. I am mostly a teetotaller, but make an exception for cases such as this one. Not that I've ever experienced this."

Millicent took the glass and dutifully walked to the small table. Instead of pouring another drink, she picked up the bottle and returned to Mrs. Hunter's side. Lifting an eyebrow, she said, "Say when."

Even under dire circumstances, Millicent always managed to make Evie smile.

Mrs. Hunter gulped down her second glass of brandy, leaned back and, closing her eyes, she sighed.

Fearing she might drop off to sleep, Evie asked, "Mrs. Hunter, when was the last time you saw Mr. Jackson?"

When Mrs. Hunter didn't respond, Evie thought she might have waited too long to ask. And, during that brief moment, she actually regretted asking because she had promised Tom she wouldn't poke around.

Millicent snapped, "Mrs. Hunter!"

"W-what? Oh… Oh, heavens." Mrs. Hunter looked at her empty glass and then at the bottle Millicent held.

Millicent took prompt action and held the bottle out of her reach. "Her ladyship wants to know when you last saw Mr. Jackson."

"He's dead."

"Yes, we've already told you that."

"Are you sure he's dead."

"The only proof we have is the fact the police are investigating."

"Oh, dear."

"Didn't you see them drive by?" Millicent turned to the window. "I'm sure you can see motor cars driving by and turning into the road that leads to Halton House. Yes, there goes a motor car."

Evie could tell the conversation was about to be steered away. Before that could happen, she said, "Mrs. Hunter, yesterday morning you left the meeting straight after Mr. Jackson. Did you speak with him?"

"Me?"

Evie saw Millicent's cheeks puff out and knew she was about to snap at Mrs. Hunter, so she hurried to explain, "Yes. You and Mr. Wiltmore left together straight after Mr. Jackson."

"Oh, no…. We didn't speak. He left in a hurry and Mr. Wiltmore and I shuffled out behind him. As the meeting had ended so abruptly, I had to decide where to go to next. I knew there was something I needed to get for my meal, but I just couldn't remember what it was."

"And Mr. Wiltmore?"

"You'll have to ask him."

They already knew Mr. Jackson had ended up at the tearoom.

Evie didn't know what else to ask without sounding too intrusive or taking advantage of Mrs. Hunter. She'd had two glasses of brandy in quick succession. Her head had to be spinning.

Sitting up, Mrs. Hunter eyed the bottle. Noticing this, Millicent held it out of her reach again. "What about later in the day? Did you see him?" Once again, Millicent looked toward the window.

If Mr. Jackson had made his way along the road, Mrs. Hunter might have seen him.

Evie remembered noticing the way his coat had appeared to be pulled up. If he had been killed nearby and then dragged out of sight, then he might have made his way along the road and toward the place where he would be killed. The police would need conclusive evidence of that. Otherwise, they'd have to consider the possibility he'd been killed somewhere else and then taken to the woods.

"Oh, dear. My apologies, I'm very upset." Struggling to her feet, Mrs. Hunter straightened her clothes. "I appreciate you coming by and letting me know. However, I need some time to process this."

Evie explained their reason for the visit had nothing to do with Mr. Jackson's death. "At the risk of sounding insensitive, we need to continue with the preparations for the pageant."

"Do you think it would be proper?"

"Mrs. Hunter, the children have been looking forward to it."

"Of course. Perhaps tomorrow…"

"Yes, we'll return tomorrow."

"Very well." Mrs. Hunter reached for the bottle.

Sighing, Millicent said, "Consider drowning your sorrows in a cup of tea."

CHAPTER 12

The game is indeed afoot

The village

Walking out of Mrs. Hunter's cottage, Evie glanced over her shoulder and saw her standing at the window, peering out, almost as if Mrs. Hunter wished to make sure they left.

When they reached the motor car, Evie smiled at Edmonds. "We're back sooner than expected. Have you seen anything interesting?"

"The streets have been unusually quiet, my lady."

Evie glanced up and down the lane and the street beyond. She didn't see anyone out and about. How odd. She assumed word had already spread and had no trouble imagining everyone peering through their windows to keep track of proceedings.

Somehow, someone had found out about her clash with Mr. Jackson and had delivered the news to Halton House. She had no idea how that had happened. However, whatever means had been employed could just as easily be used to spread word about an unexpected death in the village.

When they settled in, Edmonds asked, "Where to now, my lady?"

"We're going to see Mr. Wiltmore. He lives just behind the church. I think it's three houses down. I'm just not sure on which side of the street it is."

"It's the house with the blue door," Millicent chirped.

As they headed to their next destination, Millicent glanced at Evie and quickly looked away. After several more glances, she shrugged and asked, "I wonder if anyone in the village knows about Mrs. Hunter's drinking problem."

"Now, now, Millicent, we mustn't jump to conclusions."

"Milady, the sherry bottle was nearly empty. I'm not surprised she asked for brandy. It was three quarters full, meaning she'd already enjoyed one quarter, but there was plenty more to enjoy. When we return tomorrow, I wouldn't be surprised to find the bottle nearly empty."

Evie hid her smile. "Still, we don't know all the facts. Mrs. Hunter might entertain a great deal."

"No, she doesn't. I've heard say that after a lifetime of being in a classroom full of young ones, she rather prefers her own company." Millicent grinned. "Of course, we now know she's not entirely alone."

"Is there anything I can say to discourage you from entertaining those assumptions about Mrs. Hunter?"

"You could try to order me to stop, but I'd still think the thoughts. I'm just fascinated by the way people present themselves in public and then behave so differently in private. You can't really say that about me. I'm the same, no matter where I happen to find myself."

Evie couldn't argue with that. Even if Millicent disguised herself as her cousin, thrice removed, she'd still be herself. Although, she'd probably be more mindful of her accent. Or perhaps not. No, she would find a way to work it into the charade and remain true to herself. An original and quite authentic.

"I suppose I should apologize to Mr. Winchester," Evie murmured.

"Whatever for?" Millicent asked.

"I can't really remember the details of our brief conversation after luncheon, but I'm sure I promised I wouldn't prod around for information."

"Milady, you couldn't help asking Mrs. Hunter questions. That reminds me. I think Mrs. Hunter saw us approaching the house and threw on her coat and pretended to be rushing out to post a letter. She didn't have her handbag and her coat pockets were tiny, certainly not big enough to fit an envelope in. As you said, we don't know all the facts. I just can't help thinking that, in her haste, she might have forgotten to pick it up. Then again, I didn't see any envelopes lying about. Although, I noticed a piece of paper in the fireplace. I think she might have been disposing of something. I'm sure that has nothing to do with the letter she wanted to post."

Evie stared at Millicent, her eyebrows curved up in

surprise. Millicent never ceased to amaze her. "You noticed all that? I'm glad you were observant. I was focused on deciding if I should ask Mrs. Hunter some pertinent questions."

"You must be glad you asked her about Mr. Jackson."

Had they learned anything from her reaction and response? What if Mrs. Hunter had wanted to bide her time until she could speak with Mr. Wiltmore so they could get their story straight? Her response had been rather vague. Could they believe she hadn't spoken to Mr. Jackson after leaving the meeting?

"Millicent, how did you interpret Mrs. Hunter's answers?"

"At first, I thought she would faint, but then she revived herself with the brandy and managed to answer some questions. Did she reveal anything? I don't know." Millicent frowned. "She made sure to let us know she hadn't spoken with Mr. Jackson. Can we believe her? Maybe we can. I noticed she didn't commit to an answer about whether or not she'd seen Mr. Jackson. I think she did see him and I can imagine her telling Pumpkin to look away because Mr. Jackson was walking by and looking at him would give Pumpkin nightmares because he's quite a vile creature. And, in case you're wondering, I think she talks to Pumpkin the way you and I talk to people."

"Anything is possible, Millicent."

Evie remember the stray thought she'd had.

Butter wouldn't melt in her mouth.

She told Millicent about it and had to explain how Tom had restricted his cousins to one subject each.

"Why?"

"Mr. Winchester wanted to discourage his cousins

from talking about the case and getting carried away. He's desperate to keep them out of trouble."

"Yes, but his tactics seem rather extreme. Are you saying Nathaniel could only talk about butter?" Millicent laughed. "I'm sorry I missed that."

Evie took a moment to remember her train of thought. *Butter wouldn't melt in her mouth...* Mrs. Hunter had always come across as being under control. The trait would have suited her chosen profession of teacher. Her concern for her pupils had appeared sincere, kind, and even generous. Evie couldn't imagine her pretending to care. Yet, the possibility certainly existed.

Had she been misleading?

Even the way she'd acted during the meeting might have been misleading.

"My point is that Mrs. Hunter has always expressed her views and opinions during our meetings."

"You're right. Yesterday, she was all meek and compliant," Millicent said. "Almost as if she was afraid of Mr. Jackson."

Or pretending to be afraid and actually biding her time until she could set matters straight and get rid of someone who'd become an impediment.

Evie puzzled over the thought. Had Mrs. Hunter resented Mr. Jackson for imposing his will on her?

"And what did you think about Mrs. Hunter before yesterday?" Evie asked.

Millicent took her time pondering the question. "No nonsense. She went about her business and she never lingered anywhere longer than she had to. That means she never became embroiled in village gossip or petty dramas. I've never heard anything about her spreading rumors or malicious gossip." Millicent shrugged. "Maybe that was her way of hiding her drinking problem."

"How odd."

"What, milady?"

"That I should think of that phrase. Why would I think butter wouldn't melt in her mouth?"

"It might be your intuition telling you something. You should trust it. After all, before today, we didn't know about Mrs. Hunter's drinking problem."

The motor car slowed down. Looking up, Evie realized they were not on the road leading to the church. "Edmonds?"

Edmonds brought the motor car to a stop and turned. "My lady, I thought I should take the precaution of driving around. As we were headed to the church, I saw a police vehicle headed down that road. I hope I wasn't wrong in thinking you wished to avoid encountering the detective."

Thanking Edmonds, Evie considered their next move. Would it be so bad if the detective found out she was going to visit Mr. Wiltmore? She had a legitimate excuse for calling on him and, of course, she would use the opportunity to ask a few pertinent questions. Why not do it right under the detective's nose?

Evie nudged her coat sleeve and looked at the time. Their visit to Mrs. Hunter had been cut short. At some point, they'd need to return to Halton House, but certainly not before speaking with Mr. Wiltmore.

"Edmonds, please drive us to the end of the main street, opposite the railway station." They couldn't linger by the side of the road. If she gave the detective an hour, she would have to find something to do so as not to draw attention.

"Milady? Do you have a plan?"

"Not really. I just thought we'd wander around and go to a couple of stores. I might need something from the haberdasher. Some ribbon for the garlands. Yes, some ribbon." That would be their excuse for being in the village. She already had a valid reason since the pageant still needed to be organized but it wouldn't hurt to have another excuse to fall back on.

Millicent smiled. "And while we're there, we can ask if they know about Mr. Jackson."

"It's lovely to know we are on the same page." Mrs. Hunter had said she hadn't heard about Mr. Jackson's death. Evie didn't know if they could take her word for it. But why would she lie? Shaking her head, she decided she wouldn't jump to conclusions or even make any hasty assumptions. At least, not until they knew more. "Drive on, Edmonds."

The chauffeur tipped his cap and drove them back toward the village main street.

There were several motor cars parked outside the railway station. Evie looked at the time and thought there would be a train arriving soon.

"We shouldn't be too long, Edmonds."

Pulling up her collar, Evie straightened her coat and they made their way to Mrs. Larson's Bits & Bobs.

Opening the front door, their entrance was announced by the tinkling of a dainty doorbell. There were two women at the counter and they both turned to see the new arrivals. Smiling at them, they then turned and resumed their conversation.

Evie suspected their voices had only now lowered. That made her wonder what they were talking about.

They didn't have to wait too long for Mrs. Larson to approach and ask if they needed assistance.

Evie looked around the store and, despite knowing where the ribbons were kept, she said, "We are looking for some ribbon."

"Any particular color, my lady?"

"Yes, we'd like some red ribbon."

"We have two widths to choose from. This way, please."

Weaving their way through the store, Evie decided she would comment on the festive season and mention the garlands they were making. That would create an opening for her to say something about the misfortune of losing the headmaster at the school.

"Here we are. There are two shades of red. Bright red and dark red."

Evie leaned in and expressed delight at both colors. As she straightened, she readied herself to ask her opening question. However, Millicent beat her to it. Again.

"Have you heard about Mr. Jackson?"

Mrs. Larson gave a brisk nod. "Robbie, the baker's son, came in to deliver some bread and told us he saw the police motor car drive by and thought there might be some trouble up at the big house. He said it had to be one of the Winchester lads because they were bound to get up to no good, even though they look perfectly respectable." Belatedly, Mrs. Larson realized what she'd said right in front of Evie. "Begging your pardon, my lady."

"No need to apologize, Mrs. Larson. My cousins can be rather a handful. But they mean well." Lowering her voice, Evie asked, "So what did you hear about Mr. Jackson?"

"Well, after Robbie alerted us, we kept an eye on the street and, sure enough, we saw an ambulance drive by at great speed. In no time, it was driving back. Except, this time, they were driving slowly. As if they were in no hurry. So then, Arthur, the delivery boy from the post office, came in to deliver a letter and he said he'd been cycling by and when he saw the ambulance, he made his way up the path in the woods, making sure he remained hidden. That's when he saw the body being lifted up onto the ambulance."

Intrigued, Millicent asked, "So how did you know it was Mr. Jackson?"

"I didn't, until Mr. Barnaby, the fellow who delivers the milk and butter to the tearoom, came in because his wife had asked him to pick up a parcel I'd prepared for her, and he said he'd been on his way to deliver some cheese at the pub when he saw the police at Mr. Jackson's house. It was the strangest thing, he said, because they had the keys to his house. Why would the police have keys to his house? Obviously, because something dreadful had happened to Mr. Jackson. It makes sense. Especially when you tie it all in with the speeding ambulance which then made its way back in no particular hurry. Don't you agree?"

Millicent gave a vigorous nod, clearly having no trouble following and understanding what Mrs. Larson had said. While Evie looked on feeling rather slow-witted. It seemed Mr. Barnaby, the delivery man, had put two and two together. How much more would they be able to work out if they had seen the actual scene of the crime?

"What do you think happened to him?" Mrs. Larson asked. "I can't say I'm surprised he's dead. The man came across as being quite nasty and disagreeable. Some might say he had airs about him and thought himself too good for the likes of us."

Evie had visited the haberdashery store many times and she couldn't remember Mrs. Larson ever being so chatty or opinionated.

"We don't know," Millicent said. "Although, we have it on good authority that he was hit on the head."

"Oh, my goodness. I wonder how that happened? Do you think he fell or do you think someone actually hit him, or worse, bashed his head on the ground?"

Millicent lowered her voice to a conspiratorial whisper, "We believe he was murdered."

"Oh, my goodness. By whom?"

"By a killer, of course."

"You mean to say there is a killer among us?"

"There must be."

Mrs. Larson's eyes widened. "But who would have cause to kill him? He must have done something. Do you think he did something? Yes, he must have. Otherwise, why would someone kill him? I know I often felt like telling him what for. We only crossed paths a couple of times, but that was enough to sense something nasty about him."

"I only met him the one time and I had the same urge." Millicent looked at Evie and nodded as if to encourage her to share her own experience.

Instead, Evie pointed to the red ribbons and said, "We'll take one of each, please."

As Mrs. Larson took care of wrapping the ribbons, Millicent whispered, "What's wrong?"

Offering a smile, Evie waited until they were outside to explain, "It might not be a good idea to let people know about my clash with Mr. Jackson."

"Oh, dear. Of course, you're right. Word would spread in no time and people would start pointing the finger of suspicion at you."

Looking up, Evie saw Edmonds crossing the street. When he reached them, he opened the passenger door and waited until he climbed in to say, "You won't believe what I just heard." He nudged his head toward the railway station and continued, "I crossed over to stretch my legs and the station master saw me and came over to ask how Lady Henrietta was and how he hoped she wasn't in any trouble. That's when I asked what he meant and he told me what happened yesterday when they got off the train and asked to use the telephone to contact the house."

"What happened?" Evie asked, her breath catching in her throat.

"Her ladyship gave Mr. Jackson a good walloping with her walking cane."

CHAPTER 13

Henrietta delivers a blow

The village

*H*enrietta had struck Mr. Jackson?
Millicent frowned and scolded Edmonds, "You don't need to look so pleased."

"Really? Are you going to tell me you don't find it all amusing. Just try to picture the scene with Lady Henrietta swinging her walking cane and whacking Mr. Jackson on the head with it."

Despite smiling, Millicent demanded, "Why would she do that? You can't believe everything you hear. Are there any other witnesses?"

"No, all the passengers had already made their way out of the station."

"And what was Mr. Jackson doing there?"

"I didn't ask."

Evie cringed. She now understood the reasons for Henrietta's unusual behavior. She'd been trying to hide the altercation from her. Interrupting them, Evie asked, "And Toodles knows about it?"

Edmonds nodded. "Of course. She was there and Lady Sarah was also there."

They were all in on it and had formed a conspiracy of silence.

For all she knew, Henrietta might have employed diversionary tactics. Evie remembered her unusual response to the news about them finding a body. Soon after, a commotion had broken out and the Winchester brothers had stormed the drawing room.

At the time, she'd wondered how they had found out about them discovering a body, something that had stirred them into action. She'd suspected Henrietta of spreading the news.

Had she?

Yes, most likely.

Evie closed her eyes and recalled walking into the drawing room to break the news to Henrietta about finding a body. Had Henrietta already decided she wouldn't tell her about her encounter with Mr. Jackson?

"Milady, Lady Henrietta probably forgot to tell you, what with one thing and another."

"Millicent, in case you forgot, Henrietta was the first person to hear the news. She should have told me about her altercation when I broke the news to her. It's not the sort of thing that slips your mind."

Millicent looked up the way one did when trying to recall something. "Oh. Yes, of course. She should have said, oh, dear heavens. It can't surely be a coincidence. My goodness gracious me. You'll never believe what happened at the station. Sarah, Toodles, and I had been desperately trying to contact the house when that horrible man approached us and delivered a nasty diatribe. Oh, Evangeline, you should have heard him. I've never seen or heard anyone speak the way he did to us. I thought he might strike us. So I raised my cane to defend us." Millicent drew in a long breath and nodded. "But she didn't say any of that. Maybe her ladyship was in shock. Remember, you couldn't make sense of her reaction. She walked away without asking for details about the body we found. It must have been a double shock as I imagine she was upset about her clash and then, there you were, telling her Mr. Jackson was dead." Millicent gaped. "Oh. Oh, my goodness. What if Lady Henrietta killed him?"

"Millicent! Calm down. If you recall, I only told her we'd found a body. I didn't even hint at the possible that it might be Mr. Jackson."

Good heavens. What if Millicent was right and Henrietta had killed him? Evie turned to Edmonds. "Can you repeat exactly what the station master said?"

"He chortled."

Millicent snapped. "He found it funny?"

"I was going to say, he chortled and then said, you won't believe what happened here yesterday. It was that type of chortling. It wasn't laughter. It was incredulity. Have you never chortled with incredulity?"

Millicent scoffed. "What utter silliness. You know there are people who won't abide by such silliness."

Edmonds chortled.

"Are you mocking me? This is serious. Lady Henrietta might be responsible for killing Mr. Jackson."

"How so?" Edmonds asked.

Millicent employed her unique style and reasoning to explain, "She might have caused some sort of damage to his head when she struck him, and... and he wandered off and became lost, and eventually ended up near the woods, and... and... well, and someone drove by and Mr. Jackson collapsed from his injury and fell right in front of the motor car, and the driver thought he'd killed him, so in a moment of panic he dragged him into the woods and hid him there."

Edmonds grinned. "What utter silliness."

Millicent's cheeks puffed out.

Evie patted Millicent's hand. "Calm down, dear. Henrietta might be frightened of the consequences. I'm sure she didn't cause more than a slight bruising. Think about it. Is she really strong enough to wield her walking cane and strike a tall man in the prime of his life with enough force to actually cause a fatal wound?"

Millicent took a moment to think about it. Then she turned to Edmonds. "Did her ladyship really hit Mr. Jackson? She might have tried and missed."

"I'm afraid she actually landed a blow, and she might have tried to hit him again but the station master intervened."

"What?" Evie struggled to picture the scene.

Edmonds nodded. "He rushed out of his office and tried to encourage Mr. Jackson to come in and sit down so he could recover from the blow, but Mr. Jackson refused."

Closing her eyes, Evie asked, "And then what happened?"

"Mr. Jackson staggered away and then her ladyships and Toodles left. The station master said he saw them climbing a hay cart."

Evie looked toward the railway station and thought she would like to speak with the station master herself. While she trusted Edmonds to have related the story word for word, she needed to know about the circumstances.

If Henrietta had struck Mr. Jackson, she must have been provoked.

Now the scene took shape in her mind with practically no effort from her. Yes, she could easily imagine Mr. Jackson delivering a rude remark and Henrietta reacting to it. But why would Henrietta omit to tell them about the ordeal? She should have said something straight after she told her about finding the body. Instead, Henrietta had chosen to avoid the subject altogether.

Checking the time, she decided to postpone the conversation with the station master. They needed to speak with Mr. Wiltmore.

Hoping the police had finished their interview, she directed Edmonds to drive them to his house.

"What do you think happened, milady?"

"I cannot even begin to imagine, Millicent."

"What was Mr. Jackson doing at the station? He must have said something to provoke her ladyship. Unless, of course…"

"What?"

"No, never mind."

Evie encouraged Millicent. "Come on, I'm curious."

"Well, it's possible her ladyship has… you know… gone a bit funny in the head. She is rather eccentric. At least, that's how we see her. Others might have different opinions on the matter and might even think she shouldn't be allowed out in public." Millicent shrugged. "Then again, Mr. Jackson had shown himself to be quite rude. Yes, he must have said something to set her ladyship off, like a trigger. Which brings me back to her ladyship not being quite right in the head. At this point, I feel I should apologize if I overstepped my mark."

"No need, Millicent. It's only an opinion and we should always be open to different opinions. Even the ones we don't care for."

The moment Edmonds turned into the street running alongside the church, Evie craned her neck and identified the police motor car, but only because a constable stood next to it.

Edmonds slowed down. "My lady? Would you like me to drive on?"

"No, Edmonds. That won't be necessary." She almost changed her mind when she saw the detective making his way out of the house.

Detective Inspector Everett looked up and straight at them, following their progress as Edmonds brought the vehicle to a stop on the opposite side of the street.

"We have nothing to hide," Evie murmured. "In fact, we are within our rights to visit Mr. Wiltmore. Come along, Millicent. We have some Christmas pageant business to discuss with Mr. Wiltmore."

Stepping out of the vehicle, Evie took her time

straightening her coat while casting furtive glances at the detective who was actually taking his time getting into the motor car and, no doubt, casting furtive glances their way.

They crossed the street and, at the last minute, Evie looked up and had to acknowledge the detective.

"Lady Woodridge and Miss Peters."

Evie couldn't tell anything by his tone. She now expected him to launch into a tirade about people meddling in police business and warning her to stay away.

"Detective. I assume you've been to see Mr. Wiltmore. We have some school business with him. I do hope he's up to sitting down for a chat."

"School business?"

"Yes. The Christmas pageant is coming up and we mustn't disappoint the children. They've been looking forward to it. It's the highlight of the season for them. I'm sure I mentioned it to you earlier. We are putting on a performance."

"Indeed." He studied her for a moment, before asking, "Is that all you're here to discuss?"

"To be perfectly honest, I'm sure we'll end up talking about Mr. Jackson." Evie shrugged. "One never knows where a conversation will lead." Smiling, Evie looked at her watch. "We mustn't keep you. I'm sure you have many people to interview."

The detective tipped his hat and, to Evie's surprise, stepped aside and gestured to the house.

When they reached the door, Evie whispered, "He's still there, watching us. I can sense him."

"I don't dare look over my shoulder," Millicent whispered back. "I wouldn't be surprised to find him still standing there when we come out."

Evie knocked on the door but it seemed ages before it was opened.

"Lady Woodridge and Miss Peters. Was I expecting you?"

Mr. Wiltmore looked over their shoulders. When he nodded and smiled, Evie knew he was looking at the detective.

"Mr. Wiltmore, may we come in?" Evie felt awkward asking. While she didn't wish to start on the wrong foot, the fact he hadn't invited them in suggested he didn't want to. "We have some business to discuss."

"Business?"

"The Christmas pageant."

"Are we still doing that?"

"Of course."

His features tightened. Appearing to come to some sort of decision, he invited them in, albeit reluctantly. "Then I suppose you should come in."

Good heavens. Had Mr. Jackson's abrupt manner rubbed off on Mr. Wiltmore?

He led them through to the drawing room. As Evie entered, her gaze went straight to the windows facing the street and she saw the detective still standing there and making no effort to hide the fact.

The drawing room surprised Evie. She had expected to find a room decorated to suit a man's taste. Taking her seat, she looked around the light filled room with dainty furniture and glass cabinets filled with trinkets.

On closer inspection, she suspected they might prove to be valuable pieces but only because everything else in the room seemed to be of good quality. There didn't appear to be a single item out of place. A still-life painting of flowers hung over the fireplace and a round table near the windows had an arrangement of flowers that could not possibly have come from a garden. They simply looked too perfect and Evie was sure they were hot house blooms.

Millicent sat next to her. Taking out her notebook and uncapping her fountain pen, she then looked around the room and took some notes. Evie wouldn't be surprised to later learn she had made similar observations about the room.

"What exactly did you wish to discuss? The arrangements have been made."

Evie realized he'd made no reference to Mr. Jackson. The police had just interviewed him. Why would he avoid something so obvious?

"If you recall, I did not agree with Mr. Jackson's choices." Looking down at her hands, she then said, "I'm sure you've heard about Mr. Jackson."

He blinked a couple of times before giving a reluctant nod. "Yes, a rather unfortunate business."

"I assume Detective Inspector Everett was just here to talk to you about it."

He hesitated. "Yes, he had some questions."

When he didn't reveal the content of the conversation, Evie wondered if he had been warned against discussing the matter. "I suppose you mentioned our meeting yesterday." Evie looked toward the window. "I see the detective is still out there. I'm surprised he hasn't rushed off to speak with Mrs. Hunter."

"Why would he do that?"

"Because you, Mrs. Hunter and I were probably the last people to see Mr. Jackson alive."

His cheeks colored.

"Did you happen to mention the disagreement I had with Mr. Jackson?"

Mr. Wiltmore shifted in his seat. "Where are my manners. May I offer you some tea?"

"Thank you. That would be lovely." Evie had no great desire to drink tea, but she wanted to take the opportunity to look around the room. Hopefully, Mr. Wiltmore would need to step out of the room to organize the tea.

"I won't be long."

As soon as he left, Evie looked out the window. The police vehicle had now gone.

"What do you make of that?" Millicent whispered. "He wants to pretend as if nothing's happened. I find that suspicious. Don't you?"

"Yes." Evie stood up and walked around the room, taking her time to inspect all the items on display. "I was right," she whispered. She studied a small case encrusted with flowers carved out of mother of pearl and other semi precious stones. Even to Evie's untrained eye, it looked like a Japanese design and quite valuable at that. Not exactly the sort of trinket one would expect to find in an otherwise modest house.

There were several miniature portraits of people dressed in clothes from the 17th century. At one time, they had been quite popular but only with people who could afford to have their portraits painted.

A small glass topped cabinet housed a collection of snuff boxes, all displaying intricate designs and excellent craftsmanship.

This was quite a bounty on full display. It surprised Evie because they appeared to be quite valuable. Anyone could break in and steal them.

The door opened and Mr. Wiltmore returned.

"As I was saying," Evie began, "did you tell the detective about my altercation with Mr. Jackson?"

He nodded. "The detective asked me to describe the meeting and was quite pushy about it. He wanted to know everything."

"Did you tell him you and Mrs. Hunter followed Mr. Jackson out of his office?"

"I told him Mr. Jackson brought the meeting to a close and the detective didn't ask any further questions, so I didn't feel the need to elaborate."

The door opened. Turning, Mr. Wiltmore said, "Here's Anna with the tea."

Anna?

Evie glanced at Millicent. She couldn't be sure, but she thought Millicent had said Anna worked for Mr. Jackson. Was it a coincidence? Perhaps it was another Anna.

Mr. Wiltmore poured the tea. Accepting the cup, Evie studied the fine porcelain and intricate design and knew this was no ordinary bit of crockery.

As she sipped her tea, Evie glanced at the painting hanging over the fireplace. She was about to look away when she noticed the tulips. Her last governess had been quite passionate about art and Evie remembered her explaining how the Dutch had valued tulips in the 1600s. While Evie wouldn't begrudge Mr. Wiltmore owning a valuable painting, she had to wonder how he could afford it.

Distracted, she asked, "Did you see Mr. Jackson again during the day?"

"Yes, but only from a distance. I saw him heading toward the railway station."

Oh, dear.

That must have been right before his altercation with Henrietta. And now they knew there was another witness who could place Mr. Jackson at the station.

Shaking her head, Evie remembered to ask about Mr. Jackson's letters of reference. With any luck, it might provide some information about Mr. Jackson's life. And, with real luck, he still had it in his possession. For all she knew, Mr. Wiltmore might have brought it to the detective's attention.

Mr. Wiltmore's cheeks colored. "There were a couple."

"And did you follow up on them?"

He nodded. "I took one and Mrs. Hunter took the other. We were in a hurry to fill the position so we thought it best to divide the task."

"Do you still have the letter?" It would have been remiss of him to misplace it or dispose of it.

He hesitated. Closing his eyes briefly, he pushed out a breath and nodded.

"May I see it, please?"

"Of course. If I can find it."

"Do please try."

She watched Mr. Wiltmore hunt through several drawers until, with obvious reluctance, he drew an envelope out of a bottom drawer.

"Here it is." He stared at it for a long moment before handing it over.

"Thank you. May I take it?"

Again, she saw a hint of reluctance. However, he again nodded.

Evie put the letter away in her handbag. Setting her cup down, she thanked him for his time, and stood up.

Millicent looked surprised, as did Mr. Wiltmore.

"I thought you wished to discuss the Christmas pageant," he said.

"Mrs. Hunter is expecting us tomorrow," Evie explained. "Perhaps we can meet at her house and make our way to the school. Would the afternoon suit?"

Mr. Wiltmore drew in a deep breath and nodded.

"Wonderful. I'll send a note to Mrs. Hunter letting her know. Thank you for your time, Mr. Wiltmore."

Outside, Millicent waited until they were well out of hearing to say, "Milady, did you notice something?"

"I'm not sure. Oh, before I forget. Was that the Anna who worked for Mr. Jackson?"

"Yes. I had no idea she also worked for Mr. Wiltmore."

"I wonder if we can suspect her of spreading the word about my clash with Mr. Jackson? Is she the type to gossip?"

"She most certainly is. In fact, I wouldn't be surprised to learn she'd pressed her ear to the door and heard everything you said."

Crossing the street, Evie thought she heard whistling. She looked up the street and then down the street and saw a man in a suit walking away, his hands in his pockets, his hat tipped back.

Was he really whistling?

He was…

Edmonds held the passenger door open. As Evie

turned to climb in, she recalled the name of the other detective.

Detective Constable Jenkins.

Tom had said he whistled.

Had he been hovering nearby, waiting to see if and when they came out of Mr. Wiltmore's house? Yes, she had no trouble imagining Detective Inspector Everett asking him to hover around and keep an eye on that troublesome Countess of Woodridge.

They'd been spied on!

CHAPTER 14

Following the trail of breadcrumbs

The village

Evie drew out the letter Mr. Wiltmore had given her and looked at the name written on the envelope. "We'll have to contact Mr. Saunders. He might be able to tell us something about Mr. Jackson's previous position. If he gave a good reference, then he had no reason to let Mr. Jackson's behavior influence him."

"Is that good or bad?" Millicent asked.

"To be perfectly honest, I don't know. What I do know is that Mr. Jackson seemed to have a way about him."

"Meaning, he could make people cower."

"Yes."

"Do you think Mr. Jackson had the same influence on Mr. Saunders?"

There was only one way Evie could answer that honestly. She read the letter once and then again. As expected, Mr. Saunders had provided a glowing report and recommendation.

What would he say in person?

Evie showed Millicent the letter and waited for her appraisal.

When she finished, Millicent smiled. "How do we know Mr. Jackson didn't write this himself?"

"You read my thoughts, Millicent. If Mr. Saunders sings his praises, I'll try to think of a way to get the information out of him. Sometimes, it's not so much what someone says but rather what they don't say or what they try to avoid saying."

Evie remembered her reasoning after clashing with Mr. Jackson. To her surprise, she still believed it.

To be fair to Mr. Jackson, his rudeness might have been temporary and the result of personal issues or circumstances beyond his control.

Evie hoped Mr. Saunders might be able to cast some light on his past life which would either confirm his behavior as a personal trait or discredit it and excuse it as a temporary affliction.

In which case, Evie hoped it was nothing more serious than a young woman declining Mr. Jackson's offer of marriage. That could sour anyone's temperament.

"And what about Anna? Should we have a friendly chat with her?" Millicent asked.

Evie smiled. "A friendly chat? Why do you make it sound sinister?"

"A friendly chat with a serious edge. That seems to be the only way to get some real information. Issue an underlying threat, one replete with dire repercussions."

Evie laughed. "Have you been practicing that line?"

Grinning, Millicent admitted to indulging in a few flights of fancy while Mr. Wiltmore tried to evade her questions. "At one point, I wanted to shake him."

"Well, I'm glad it didn't come to that. As for the rest, we'll play it by ear." Evie instructed Edmonds to drive on.

As they crossed the village, she looked toward the railway station and wondered if she should divert Edmonds.

Settling back, Evie decided they had done enough for one day. Tomorrow, they would need to return and meet with Mrs. Hunter and Mr. Wiltmore and discuss what they would do for the Christmas pageant. She only knew they needed a new theme to make the children's Christmas pageant special.

Millicent brought out her notebook and read through what she'd written.

Evie watched her close the notebook and, no doubt, toss about what she'd just read. She saw Millicent glance at her once and then again, before she finally drew her attention to what she wanted to say by tapping her notebook.

"During our visit to Mr. Wiltmore, I took some notes of my observations. They seem frivolous, but at the time I thought it might be important."

Evie smiled. "Did you happen to notice the fine furnishings?"

Millicent gasped. "Milady! Are you saying you noticed the quality of the furniture?"

"I did."

"So did I. It was very fine. Not as good as the furnishings at Halton House, yet still quite impressive. I know Mr. Wiltmore is a retired solicitor, but he worked in the country. I'm sure if he'd worked in town he might have earned a lot more. I just don't understand how he could afford all that. I suppose there's the possibility he inherited some pieces."

Evie nodded. "Are you suggesting we look into Mr. Wiltmore's business dealings?"

"We believe Mr. Jackson was killed. Are there any suspects?" Millicent shook her head. "So far, I haven't heard a single one mentioned. Doesn't that strike you as odd?"

Evie wondered if she'd been trying to avoid the subject because, in reality, she was the only one who might have a motive, and there were witnesses to prove it.

"Do you think Mr. Wiltmore had reason to want to see Mr. Jackson dead?" Evie asked. She had her own idea on the matter, but she wanted to hear what Millicent had to say.

Millicent looked down at her notebook. After a moment, she smiled. "How did he behave with us when we just visited him?"

"That's a valid point, Millicent. He looked quite confident and I remember thinking he might have acquired Mr. Jackson's rudeness."

"Exactly. His behavior with us today was the complete opposite of what we saw yesterday. Whatever Mr. Jackson did to make Mr. Wiltmore cower might be reason enough to make Mr. Wiltmore a suspect."

What reason could he possibly have to want to kill Mr. Jackson?

The country solicitor had never struck Evie as being unbalanced. He'd always been polite, at least, until a short while before. Then again, the circumstances had been strenuous. The police had just been to his house and he might have felt rattled by the experience.

Evie shook her head. She really ought to stop making excuses for people's bad behavior. There was never any good reason for treating anyone with rudeness.

How on earth did Mr. Jackson wield so much power? Did he have something hanging over Mr. Wiltmore and Mrs. Hunter?

"You're right, Millicent. We should consider Mr. Wiltmore a suspect."

"And Mrs. Hunter?"

Evie laughed. "You asked that with so much enthusiasm, I'm tempted to say you actually want her to be the killer."

"Oh, I think it would be tremendous fun to corner her and accuse her of killing Mr. Jackson."

"Millicent! It could drive the woman to drink."

"Precisely. I wonder if she's a happy drunk. Oh, there's a thought. Remember, Mr. Wiltmore was not the only one who cowered. Mrs. Hunter was just as bad. They were both frightened of Mr. Jackson."

"Millicent. Don't let Mr. Winchester know this, but you have a wonderful talent for this sleuthing business, as good if not better than Mr. Winchester's observations."

"Millicent Peters, lady's maid, private secretary and lady detective with supreme sleuthing abilities. I like the sound of that. I could set up my own agency and go into competition with Lotte Mannering. First, I'll have to gain experience. So I suppose I could work for her. Oh… and you, of course. I always forget you are both in business together." Millicent quirked her eyebrow. "I don't suppose you'd like to make me a partner."

"There's an idea. You'd be a credit to the agency. I'll propose it to Lotte and give you my full support."

"Wonderful. I suppose I'll have to start as a junior partner, what with me not actually contributing finances."

"You seem to think of everything. Well done."

They both sat back and sighed with satisfaction. However, Millicent seemed quite eager to prove herself more than she already had.

"Milady, don't you think we should speak with Mrs. Hunter again now? She must have worked her way through another quarter of a bottle of brandy. I'm sure she'll be quite agreeable."

"Millicent, I didn't know you could be so devious. But what if she's not agreeable."

"You're right. She could turn out to be a nasty drunk." Millicent fell silent but it didn't last. "Oh, there's an idea. What if, after our meeting yesterday, she became so angry at Mr. Jackson because of what he'd forced her to become that she hit the bottle and became quite inebriated. In her drunken state, she decided she would seek her revenge."

Millicent's imagination knew no bounds. She wove a tale that meandered in so many directions, Evie struggled to keep up.

Did Mrs. Hunter have it in her to kill a person, even in a drunken state?

Butter wouldn't melt in her mouth.

Killers didn't advertise their intentions. That was why

some killers managed to get away with committing their crime.

"Well done, Millicent. We now have two suspects."

Millicent ran her finger along her notebook. Lowering her voice, she said, "Milady, you seem to have forgotten the third suspect."

Yes, she had completely forgotten.

What if Henrietta's assault with her walking cane had caused significant enough damage to result in Mr. Jackson's death?

"No."

"No?"

Evie turned to Millicent. "I'm referring to your earlier suggestion. Mrs. Hunter can wait until tomorrow. Right now, we need to return to Halton House and speak with Henrietta."

CHAPTER 15

Always expect the unexpected

Halton House

As Edmonds made his way along the drive leading to Halton House, both Evie and Millicent craned their necks to look ahead. When Edmonds brought the motor car to a stop, the front door opened and Edgar stepped out and walked toward them at a normal pace.

So far, everything looked perfectly normal.

"Always expect the unexpected," Millicent murmured and cast her gaze around the house and the surrounding grounds, as if looking for something out of place.

Evie climbed out of the motor car and smiled at Edgar. He looked perfectly at ease, so she had no reason to think he was about to tell her Tom had been tied up to the highest branch of a tree, and now required the skilled assistance of a lumberjack to help bring him down.

"Edgar, I trust all is well at Halton House. It's still standing."

"Yes, my lady. For once, I have nothing to report or warn you about."

"Marvelous. We should celebrate."

Edgar glanced back at the house. To Evie's surprise, he looked quite amused.

"Edgar? Is there something you wish to tell me?"

He shook his head and continued smiling as he led the way to the front door. Just before opening it, he turned and beamed at Evie.

Oh, dear.

A feeling of trepidation swept through her.

Evie turned to Millicent but, for once, Millicent had no idea what to say and she let her know as much by shrugging.

Edgar opened the door and made a sweeping gesture with his hand.

Oh, dear.

As they stepped inside, Evie searched the hall and saw Tom and all his cousins lounging about around the fireplace. The Christmas Tree had been installed at the far end, but it wouldn't be decorated until later in the week. While there were no rules about it, the hall was only ever used for large celebratory gatherings. At any other time, people were happy to use the drawing room or the library.

Then it began.

One by one, the Winchester brothers hummed, all joining in to sing a beloved Christmas carol.

Edgar's smile turned to satisfaction. "Mr. Winchester calls it a barbershop sextet. They spent the last hour singing because Mr. Winchester told them that was the only way you would ever forgive him. And, besides, all you ever wanted for Christmas was to have your own personal Christmas carol singers."

"Splendid." Evie turned to see if Millicent agreed and was surprised to see her looking quite disappointed. "Millicent? What's wrong?"

Rolling her eyes, Millicent said, "My hopes are dashed. All the way here, I'd been wondering what new surprise the Winchester lads had in store for us. Yes, this is nice. Albeit a little sedate. Oh, well. Perhaps next time."

The Winchester cousins finished their singing and, one by one, sat back to twiddle their thumbs.

Tom thundered, "Try to look excited when you're twiddling your thumbs."

Oh, dear.

Had Tom found another way to torture his cousins?

"Millicent, whatever you need to do now, do please hurry back. I'd like to speak with Henrietta and might need you to keep track of what is said." Evie walked across the hall and smiled as she approached the group. "That was lovely. I didn't know you could all sing."

One by one, they looked at Tom, almost as if asking for permission to speak.

"Countess, I'm glad to hear you enjoyed it. You only need to say the word and they will burst into song."

"What?"

Tom grinned. "You can make a request, any song you like."

"The Holly and the Ivy?" Evie suggested.

The Winchesters leaned in for a brief discussion. Then, standing up, they began to sing in tune.

Tom looked as pleased as Punch when he winked at Evie and mouthed, "I told you I'd whip them into shape."

When they finished, Evie praised and thanked them, and told them they could take a break.

They all looked at Tom, who took his time giving a nod of approval. He had indeed whipped them into compliance.

As Evie asked Tom to follow her to the library, she thought of someone else who had apparently wielded power over others. What means had Mr. Jackson employed to make Mrs. Hunter and Mr. Wiltmore meek and compliant?

And… Had it all backfired, with one of them reaching breaking point and taking measures to do away with Mr. Jackson?

Tom followed Evie to the library and, after closing the door behind him, said, "I trust you had a successful afternoon. What did you find out?"

Glancing over her shoulder at him, Evie shrugged. "I'm not sure I know what you mean."

Grinning, Tom said, "I'm sure you do."

"Oh, very well. But if you must know I didn't go out of my way to ask questions. The opportunities simply presented themselves."

"Opportunities? More than one?"

"What can I say? They fell on my lap."

"Isn't that always the case?"

Evie gave him a sweet smile. "I wish the detective could be as understand as you always seem to be. By the way, I wasn't going to mention it, however, Millicent deserves full credit. She has proven herself to be extremely adept at the game of sleuthing."

"Oh, so now it's a game."

"You know what I mean. Anyhow, she has the admirable ability to see things I miss, and then she weaves the most engaging tales. Best of all, she's extremely adept. Did I already mention that? Anyhow, she's so adept, she's now in line to become a junior partner in our agency."

"Are you telling me or asking for my opinion?"

"I'm telling you. You're only an honorary partner because you're a man. Millicent has the advantage of being a woman."

"There are seven Winchester men here and suddenly, we are all outnumbered by you and Millicent." Going to stand by the fireplace, he asked, "Are you going to share your findings?"

"I'm not sure where to start. Although, I did discover something extraordinary today. We called in at Mrs. Larson's Bits & Bobs for some ribbon and she told us about all the goings on in the village."

Tom's eyebrows lifted. "Do tell."

"First, there was Robbie, the baker's son. He went in to deliver some bread and told Mrs. Larson he saw the police drive by and head toward Halton House. Would you believe it? He immediately jumped to conclusions and thought it might have something to do with your cousins because they were bound to get up to no good."

Tom sighed and shook his head. "I'm trying my best, Countess."

"You're doing a splendid job, dear. Anyhow…"

"There's more?"

"Oh, yes. Arthur, the post office delivery boy, was doing his deliveries when he saw the ambulance arrive. He sneaked along the path for a closer look and saw the body being loaded into the ambulance. Then, there was Mr. Barnaby who delivers the milk. He saw the police at Mr. Jackson's house and said they let themselves in with the key. Eventually, they all reached the same conclusion and identified the victim as Mr. Jackson."

Tom gaped at her. "How?"

"By simple means of deduction. Oh, I nearly forgot. Mrs. Larson thought Mr. Jackson was nasty and disagreeable." Evie gave a firm nod. "You see, I have been vindicated. He wasn't just rude to me." Digging inside her handbag, Evie produced the letter Mr. Wiltmore had given her. "I thought I'd have to wrench it away from Mr. Wiltmore's clutches. That has to mean something." She explained about the reference letters for Mr. Jackson's appointment and her suspicion about Mr. Jackson coercing the referees into writing a glowing report about him, flattering enough to hide his true nature.

"How are you going to confirm that?"

Evie looked at the address. "He lives about an hour away. Millicent and I could set off early, visit Mr. Saunders, have luncheon along the way, and then return to meet with Mrs. Hunter and Mr. Wiltmore to sort out the Christmas pageant in the afternoon."

Tom looked worried. "What about me?"

"What about you, dear? You'll have your hands full with your cousins, who, by the way, have acquired the reputation for getting up to no good."

"Who said?"

"Mrs. Larson from Bits & Bobs and… I seem to recall you repeatedly telling me about your feral relatives."

"Yes, but it's different when I say it. Are you telling me that Mrs. Larson said that to your face."

"Yes, it's so refreshing to be able to speak freely. I wouldn't be comfortable with people always treating me with deference." Evie looked up and hummed. "Let me think, what else did we learn. Oh, that's right… Anna."

Tom's voice hitched. "Who's she?"

"Anna did house cleaning for Mr. Jackson and, today we discovered she also works for Mr. Wiltmore. Millicent and I believe she is the source of the rumors that reached Halton House about me having a disagreement with Mr. Jackson."

"Rumors?" Tom smiled. "Are you about to deny it ever happened?"

"Certainly not. Someone had to stand up to him."

Tom crossed his arms.

Trying to sound worried, Evie asked, "Oh, dear… Are you cross?"

Tom's chin lifted. As he spoke, his eyes sparkled with amusement, "Do you blame me? I feel left out."

"But you're busy. I couldn't possibly ask you to tear yourself away what with your cousins being such a handful. By the way, your creativity is to be commended. You could just as easily have tied them up for the duration of their stay. But you didn't. You're doing an excellent job with them. However… while I enjoyed the singing, Millicent felt let down. She was rather hoping to witness some excitement."

Tom growled. "You're enjoying this."

"Not as much as you seem to be enjoying bringing your cousins to heel."

Giving her a brisk smile, Tom said, "Yes, but… think of all you did in a single afternoon and all of it without me. Wait a minute, did you get around to speaking with Mrs. Hunter about the Christmas pageant? After all, that was the main purpose of your visit to the village."

"Oh, yes. Our encounter with Mrs. Hunter was wonderfully amusing. Did you know she drinks? Millicent wanted to get her drunk so she would tell us everything she knows. I never knew she could be so devious."

"Who? Millicent or Mrs. Hunter?"

"Both. You won't believe what Mrs. Hunter did. When we arrived, she pretended to be on her way out. She is definitely hiding something. We'll find out more tomorrow."

"Tomorrow? After your visit to Mr. Saunders and your luncheon and your afternoon visit to Mrs. Hunter and Mr. Wiltmore to discuss the pageant?"

"Yes, it's good to see you've been paying attention. Thank you."

"And yet I still feel left out."

"Tom, you're doing important work here. That reminds me. Have you seen Henrietta and the others?"

"Only briefly. They went out for a walk. My tribe's singing was a bit scratchy at first and they couldn't stand the racket." Tom looked toward the windows. "Here they come."

Evie stood up and went to the nearest window. Tom joined her and said, "They look as thick as thieves."

Closing her eyes, she inhaled a calming breath. Evie only now remembered the most important bit of information they had come across. Lowering her voice, she said, "There's something I meant to tell you…"

Where to start?

"Do you remember asking if I'd noticed something odd about Henrietta?"

"Oh, yes. It's not just Henrietta. Toodles and Sarah are also unusually quiet." Tom studied her for a moment. "You know something."

Evie nodded and looked at the trio cutting across the park and stopping every few steps to talk.

"When Millicent and I came out of Mrs. Larson's Bits & Bobs, we saw Edmonds crossing the street. He had walked to the railway station to stretch his legs."

"Do I need to sit down for this?" Tom asked.

"Oh, no. It's not that serious." By the time Evie finished telling him about Henrietta's clash with Mr. Jackson and how she had given him a good walloping with her walking cane, Tom was leaning against the window, his lips parted in disbelief.

"You said it wasn't serious. She hit him?"

"Yes." Evie waited to see if he would reach the same conclusion she and Millicent had come to.

He did.

Tom looked out the window. "Henrietta thinks she killed Mr. Jackson. That's why she's been so quiet."

"Maybe. I'm sure she doesn't have the physical strength to wield a cane with enough force to kill anyone."

Tom brushed the palms of his hands across his face. "Henrietta thinks she killed him."

"Yes, dear. You just said that."

"It explains the bruise on the side of Mr. Jackson's head." Tom shook his head. "Very well. We can't panic.

That walking cane is merely a decorative accessory. Henrietta mostly uses it to poke things and point at people. I've certainly never seen her leaning on it and can't imagine it being sturdy enough to cause any significant damage."

"The police might view it differently," Evie mused. "And that's what I'm afraid of. I'm sure Henrietta feels the same way and that's why she's been putting so much effort into diverting attention from herself. What are we going to do?"

Before Tom could make any suggestions, the door to the library opened and Henrietta walked in, with Toodles and Sarah following a step behind.

"Evangeline. Tom." Henrietta reached them and struck up her most imperious pose. "I have a confession to make."

CHAPTER 16

Confession is good for the soul

The library

Pointing an accusatory finger at herself, Henrietta followed the gesture with a dramatic pause.

"A confession?"

"Yes, Evangeline. A confession."

Instead of giving Henrietta her full attention, Evie gestured to a grouping of chairs opposite the fireplace and suggested sitting down. At the same time, Tom, sounding a lot like Millicent, said they needed some tea because it was nearing that time of day when everyone got together for tea and a chat, and why wait until later when they could have some tea and cake right now.

This seemed to confuse Henrietta. "Did you not hear

what I just said? I'm sure you did. In fact, you echoed my words. As I said, I have a confession to make and I have two witnesses to support my claim. Toodles and Sarah. That should suffice and provide all the credibility I need."

Looking like reluctant witnesses, Toodles and Sarah both averted their gazes.

If Evie had to guess, she'd say they both wished to be anywhere else but right there, offering support to Henrietta who, if Evie had to have another guess, had coerced them into agreeing to be witnesses.

They needed a distraction, Evie thought. Yes, they needed someone to raise a ruckus and draw everyone's attention away from this moment, disrupting it long enough for Henrietta to come to her senses and forget all about making a confession.

Despite her earlier suspicions and confusion about Henrietta's silence, Evie now found herself desperate to avoid an impossible situation, one she simply would not accept.

In a flash of inspiration, Evie said, "Henrietta, there's no need. Tom and I know all about it. In fact, we were just now discussing it."

"You were?" Startled, Henrietta hesitated. She looked at Tom and then at Evie. However, her hesitation was only momentary.

Tapping her cane on the floor, Henrietta frowned. "That won't do." She looked down and realized she was standing on the carpet. So she moved a couple of steps and tapped her cane again on the hardwood floor. This time, she seemed satisfied with the attention grabbing tap. Lifting her chin, she declared, "I will be heard."

"Henrietta, there really is no need," Evie insisted.

"I beg to differ and, before you can interrupt me again," Henrietta's voice rose to a crescendo, "I wish to confess to the heinous murder of Mr. Jackson."

At that precise moment, the door opened and Edgar walked in to announce, "Detective Inspector Everett and Detective Constable Jenkins."

"Perfect timing," Henrietta said and tapped her cane on the floor again.

Fearing Henrietta was about to confess to the authorities, Evie stepped forward and rushed to say, "Henrietta, we all know you like an audience. While I'm sure the police would love to see you rehearse your scene from the Christmas pageant we're putting on at Halton House, I think they might be keen to get on with their business."

"But I am their business."

"Dear Henrietta, I know you love the attention and the spotlight…"

Detective Inspector Everett cleared his throat. "Lady Woodridge is right. We are rather pressed for time. If we could please have a word… in private."

Toodles and Sarah seized the opportunity and hurried to assist in the matter by grabbing hold of Henrietta and nearly dragging her out of the library with her saying, "But I must be heard. I insist. It is my right to be heard. Unhand me. The both of you are conspiring to hide…"

The rest of Henrietta's accusation was muffled by Sarah's hand covering her mouth. Luckily, the detectives had already walked toward Tom and the deception was further assisted by Edgar, who took swift action and closed the library door. As this happened, a yelp was heard.

Evie looked heavenward.

Had Henrietta sunk her teeth into Sarah's hand?

"Countess, you won't believe what the detective just told me."

As she approached the group, Evie tried to discern their intentions from the way they looked and stood. If they'd been here to arrest someone, they would have been accompanied by a couple of constables, at the very least.

Detective Constable Jenkins, the man she had seen outside Mr. Wiltmore's house, appeared to be whistling under his breath, while Detective Inspector Everett looked almost downcast, yet defiant.

Did they have good news or bad news?

She looked at Tom and saw the familiar twinkle in his eyes, a sure sign of amusement. Yet his expression remained as serious as it had been when Henrietta had made her confession.

Detective Inspector Everett spoke with great reluctance. In fact, he almost choked on his words. "We've spoken with everyone in the village and…" he shook his head. "Well, there appears to be a recurring echo with everyone providing the same answers."

Oh, dear…

Had everyone pointed the finger of suspicion at one of Tom's cousins? Which one?

Brazen.

No, not him.

Clarence and Eugene.

They were the only ones who'd managed to escape Tom's whip and, despite Tom's efforts to thwart their escape, they had managed to drive quite a distance, along the way encountering Mr. Jackson.

The detective continued, "It seems no one in the village saw anything of significance."

Confused, Evie asked, "What does that mean?"

"No one saw anything out of the ordinary. Mr. Jackson was killed and taken to the woods. He didn't get there by himself. Yet no one saw anything."

"Can you be sure of that? I mean, are you sure Mr. Jackson didn't go to the woods himself?"

The detective looked surprised.

"I only ask because he might have gone to the woods. At our meeting, he mentioned the holly I'd need for the garlands, and he said it was available at the schoolhouse and in the woods. Although, he wasn't sure where in the woods. Perhaps he went there to see if there would be a sufficient supply for the garlands. So you see, he had reason to be in the woods."

The detective shook his head. "The autopsy is a mere formality. He died somewhere else."

Evie tensed. Had he died from a blow to the head and then been carried there? She considered something that hadn't occurred to her before. Even someone without much strength could land a fatal blow. It would just be a matter of hitting the right spot.

"Countess, he died somewhere else."

"What does that mean?"

When Tom didn't answer her, the detective said, "Mr. Jackson was poisoned."

"What?" Evie almost yelped the word.

"Without going into much detail, I inspected the body myself and didn't have to try hard to smell traces of almonds. The autopsy will confirm it. Anyhow, the smell of almonds is a sure sign of cyanide poisoning. The symptoms are quite severe and I didn't see any signs where the body was found."

Poisoned?

Evie tried to recall what she knew about cyanide poisoning. The detective had mentioned severe symptoms. She supposed he meant vomiting.

Evie drew in a calming breath and pushed the words out, "What about the blow to the head. Mr. Winchester said there was a bruise on the side of Mr. Jackson's head."

"I couldn't really say with any certainty. However, whoever poisoned him might also have hit him." Shrugging, he added, "The killer might have wanted to stop him from seeking help. If he recognized the symptoms he was suffering, he might have realized he'd been poisoned and, I suppose he would have tried to put up a fight. Anyhow, we know he was dragged to that precise spot in the woods by the way his coat had been pushed up."

Yes, but why the woods?

Evie eased herself down onto a chair.

Henrietta was in the clear.

Even if she'd confessed, she would not have faced any consequences. Although, there might have been lots of questions to answer.

Why had the detective come? What did he want from them?

"Countess? Did you hear that?"

"What?"

"The detective wants to know if we've heard any rumors."

Of course. The detective wanted their help. That explained his reluctance.

How very odd, she thought. He'd spoken to everyone and no one had reported seeing anything suspicious.

It was almost as if there was a conspiracy of silence among the villagers.

Sheer curiosity and daring compelled her to ask, "Did you speak with the station master?"

The detective nodded. "He said he saw the ambulance drive by but nothing else."

Nothing else?

How very odd.

If he'd told him about Henrietta's assault on Mr. Jackson, it would have been the detective's duty to get some answers.

What if the detective actually knew about the altercation and wanted to test them to see if they would share the information with him?

"Countess, didn't you mention talking with someone else who'd seen the ambulance?"

"Oh, yes. Millicent and I needed some supplies for the garlands. I'm afraid we didn't hear anything of use, and I'm not really surprised no one mentioned seeing the ambulance, other than the station master, that is. It just doesn't sound important enough. I'm actually surprised the station master didn't have more information for you. I always see him hovering around the station. He doesn't seem to have much to do until a train arrives. If anyone suspicious had traveled here by train, he would have noticed. And what about Mrs. Hunter? I assume you spoke with her."

The detective nodded. "We spoke with her, straight after speaking with Mr. Wiltmore. We then worked our way up the village, from one end to the other." He slipped his hands inside his pockets. "In your honest opinion, do you think the villagers would share information if they had any?"

"Of course. Why wouldn't they? In fact, they'd take great pride in doing so. Especially if it helped solve a case." Evie drummed her fingers on the armrest. "Was Mr. Wiltmore helpful?"

"As helpful as he could be. He told us everything he knew about Mr. Jackson and everything that happened at the meeting."

Poisoned.

Had Mr. Jackson met with someone?

Maybe the villagers were protecting one of their own. "Will the autopsy reveal how the poison was ingested?"

"Yes, of course."

"So that should somehow narrow down your choices. Only, you'll need to know where Mr. Jackson went after his lunch. Oh…"

"Lunch?"

Evie felt quite annoyed with herself. She'd been questioned only a few hours before and yet she couldn't recall if she'd mentioned seeing Mr. Jackson at lunch. So much had happened that day.

"After our meeting at the school house, Millicent and I went to the tearoom and we saw Mr. Jackson there."

"Was he with someone?"

"Not when we saw him. He sat alone at the table. Maybe someone joined him afterward."

"You didn't see?"

This was the moment of truth. "Millicent and I decided to have luncheon somewhere else."

"I see. You wished to avoid spending any time in his presence."

It wasn't a question and that annoyed Evie.

"I take it the decision was made as a result of your differences."

"Detective, I will not deny being greatly annoyed by the man. He was a bully. And a rude one at that."

"And yet we are compelled to find his killer."

"What on earth is that supposed to mean? No, no need to answer. I know perfectly well what you mean. You think we all lack sympathy for Mr. Jackson because he was rude and probably feel he deserved what he got. That is a horrid assumption."

"Indeed."

Evie and the detective locked eyes. Neither one appeared to want to be the first to look away.

Trying to diffuse the situation, Tom stepped forward. "Tea anyone?"

The drawing room

Half an hour after the detectives had left, Evie was still pacing. She had started pacing in the library and had eventually found her way to the drawing room, where she continued to pace.

When Millicent appeared, Evie snapped at her, "Where have you been?"

"Milady!"

"My apologies, Millicent. That detective has a way

about him." Evie shook her head. "Disagreeable man. And he actually expected us to help him."

"The detective was here?"

"Yes, both of them. And where were you?"

Millicent's cheeks colored. She held up her notebook. "So much happened today, I had to sit down and skim through my notebook to remind myself who said what and when and where. One of the housemaids said her ladyship was in hysterics about something or other, but I was determined to read through all my notes, and then make a few more notes because I know information can be distorted, so I tried to capture everything while it was still fresh in my mind. Has her ladyship recovered?"

"Eccentricity is not something you recover from." Evie stopped pacing and nodded. "She wanted to confess to all and sundry. Can you believe that?"

"Confess?"

"Yes, confess to killing Mr. Jackson."

Intrigued, Millicent sat down, opened her notebook and scribbled a note to herself. "Fascinating. She really thinks she is responsible for killing Mr. Jackson. What else happened?"

"We now know he died of poison."

"No. You don't say. How? Oh, do you think someone at the tearoom poisoned him?"

The thought hadn't even occurred to Evie. Or had it? Yes, it must have because the detective had asked her if she'd seen Mr. Jackson with someone...

Evie walked to the nearest chair and sat down. "Do you remember who else was at the tearoom?"

"No. The moment I saw him, I froze. Then you pulled me away and dragged me off to the next village for lunch.

I didn't blame you then and I don't blame you now. It would have been dreadfully uncomfortable to sit in the same establishment and enjoy our meal while casting furtive glances his way to see if he was looking at us. I'm sure we managed to avert disaster as it would have ended in another clash. Of course, if we had stayed, we wouldn't be asking if someone joined him for lunch because we would have seen it with our own eyes."

Surprised she had been able to follow Millicent's reasoning, Evie said, "Yes, you're right."

Tom walked in, with Holmes trotting beside him. Greeting Millicent, he then went to sit next to Evie. "Feeling better?"

Evie bent down and picked up Holmes. "No, but I'm sure Millicent will succeed in distracting me. We're trying to determine where Mr. Jackson might have been poisoned. And now I'm thinking the detective was right in thinking there's some sort of conspiracy. How is it possible no one saw him? We saw him a couple of times. And then, of course, Henrietta saw him at the station and that would have been late in the afternoon, quite possibly at about the time Millicent and I arrived back at Halton House and found you trying to contain your cousins."

Tom agreed. "Yes, it's very odd. I'm surprised the station master didn't mention Henrietta's altercation with Mr. Jackson."

"Perhaps he's being protective and knows her ladyship is not a killer," Millicent offered.

Evie gave a pensive nod. "The station master is to be commended for employing good sense. There's no point in complicating matters by telling the police something that is entirely irrelevant to the investigation."

Tom snorted. "Not relevant? Countess, Henrietta could very well have set something into motion by striking that man. He might have staggered around and lost consciousness and fallen somewhere... in the woods."

"In the woods? Are you suggesting he staggered his way to the woods?"

"He might have felt well enough to walk off his anger. He must have been furious with Henrietta. If anyone saw him, they might have assumed he was drunk."

"You're right. It is possible, but I can't believe no one saw him. The station master offered Mr. Jackson the use of his office to recuperate and he declined. When he left the station, he must have walked to his house and there's only one way there. Along the main street. Anyone out and about would have seen him."

"And yet no one came forward with information," Millicent said. "I'm actually not surprised. If I'd seen him, I would have looked away for fear I might need to acknowledge him with a nod and some sort of pleasantry such as 'My, what a lovely day it is today'. Yes, that would have been a fatal mistake because, of course, Mr. Jackson might have growled at me for entertaining such a frivolous thought. And then I might have retorted with a huff, to which he might have replied with a growl, and then..." Millicent shook her head. "No, that would not have ended well. So I'm not surprised no one saw him. They probably did, but they looked away in time to avert his attention."

It took a moment for Evie and Tom to realize Millicent had finished speaking.

A footman entered the drawing room and was surprised to find them all there. Evie realized he'd come in to tidy up before the evening.

"Don't mind us, Jon. I'm sure Edgar is about to sound the dressing gong. We'll clear the way for you now." Evie turned to Millicent. "Come along, Millicent. We can finish the conversation while I dress. And, I nearly forgot. Please send Mrs. Hunter a note saying we're meeting her tomorrow afternoon."

Tom gaped at her. "Countess?"

"Yes, dear."

"I'll take Holmes. I'm training him to herd my cousins."

CHAPTER 17

Carols by candlelight

That evening, the dining room

"Who said confessions are good for the soul? I feel enraged," Henrietta declared.

Sarah held up her injured hand. "I'm in pain. How do you think I feel? Your teeth marks are still visible."

Toodles hummed with appreciation. "This fish is delicious."

Brazen cleared his throat and delivered the first line of a song, "Jingle bells."

Wilbur followed with, "Jingle bells."

Clarence sang, "Jingle all the way."

When the song made the rounds of the table, everyone looked at Henrietta.

"I still feel enraged."

Sarah followed with, "And my hand still hurts."

"It must be Scottish fish," Toodles murmured. "It is truly delicious."

Wilbur elbowed Brazen, prompting him to start the next tune, "Silent night…"

Evie took a sip of wine and stared across the table at Tom, who looked rather pleased with himself.

Taking another sip of wine, Evie interrupted the song, which had now reached Nathaniel, "I'd like get a word in edgewise, please." She looked at Henrietta who was determined to claim the podium and issue the detailed confession she had been denied.

As Evie was about to speak, Henrietta interrupted. "There is an order to everything, and everyone is assigned a task, Evangeline. Yours is to sit back and suffer in silence. Mine is to insist on justice taking its course."

Evie cut in, saying, "Henrietta, you're right. You have been denied. Would you like us to lock you up in the attic? Or, better still, in the tower? Would that balance the scales of justice?"

"In the attic?"

"Yes. In years to come, people will wonder about your sudden disappearance. Then, someone will start a rumor about the Dowager Countess of Woodridge imprisoned in the tower."

"The mad countess," Sarah suggested. "Or just plain mad Henrietta, because I wouldn't want there to be a mix-up and have people think it's me."

Henrietta lifted her chin. "I have often thought there

are too many dowagers in this house. Then, I take comfort because I am the first dowager."

"Nonsense," Sarah scoffed. "There have been other dowagers before you. We have a whole row of their paintings, one looking more deranged than the other. We need to put your portrait up in the gallery. You'll be in fine company."

Toodles looked up and drew Edgar's attention. "This fish is really delicious. I'd like some more, please."

"On the first day of Christmas," Brazen sang.

Wilbur followed with, "My true love gave to me."

It took several rounds of the table for the song to finally reach its end with Nathaniel singing, "And a partridge in a pear tree."

Evie glanced across the table at Tom and wondered if he realized his cousins had fully embraced their punishment and were having fun.

When the meal ended, Evie left Tom with his cousins and led the others to the drawing room.

Five minutes later, she was not surprised to see Tom enter the drawing room, with his cousins piling in behind him.

"What did we miss?" Eugene asked.

Henrietta invited Eugene to sit next to her and proceeded to fill him in on her woes.

Evie had sat for a full five minutes, lost in her thoughts and doing her best to ignore Henrietta's complaints. Now, she looked up in surprise. Had the embargo been lifted? Were the Winchester brothers allowed to speak freely again?

Tom helped himself to a drink and joined her by the fireplace. "You looked lost in thought."

"That's because I was."

"How on earth do you manage that?" He looked at Henrietta. "Has she stopped talking at all?"

"No and she won't. At least, not until she runs out of words or complaints and that's not likely to happen any time soon."

"So what were you thinking about?"

"Negatives." Taking a sip of her drink, she tried to recapture the train of thought she had been entertaining. "Since first meeting Mr. Jackson, I've focused on his negative character."

"That's not unusual, Countess. People are naturally inclined to notice the negatives. If I say I like a book and someone else comes along and says it's the worst book ever, people listening will side with the person who dislikes the book."

"How very odd."

"Human nature is odd."

"Misguided and easy to persuade and manipulate?" Evie asked.

"Absolutely."

She wondered about the people holding negative opinions about Mr. Jackson. Had they all formed their opinions after meeting him or had they been influenced by what others had said about him?

"Are you still thinking about it?" Tom asked.

Evie nodded. "Yes, and I'm not getting anywhere."

"Unburden yourself, Countess."

"Very well, even if it all reflects badly on me. Before I met Mr. Jackson in person, Millicent told me he was extremely punctilious. I took her word for it and I remember feeling on edge about meeting him in person for the first time. Now that I think about it, I'm not sure why I felt on edge. What's wrong with showing attention to detail or caring about correct behavior?"

"He was rude to you," Tom reminded her. "How is that caring for correct behavior?"

"Yes, but it's all about perspective. In his mind, I was late to the meeting, but only because the others had arrived early. Anyhow, he obviously considered my tardiness a lapse in manners."

"That sounds twisted."

"It is but, as I said, it's all about perspective and personal viewpoints. From where he stood, I had failed to be punctual. Now that I think about it, it's possible that the way he conducted the meeting had been influenced by rumors he heard about me."

Tom's eyebrows shot up. "I'm intrigued to hear the rest. Do you think someone has been spreading rumors about you?"

"I'm sure, at some point, everyone becomes the subject of conversation and personal opinions."

"And what do you think Mr. Jackson heard about you?"

"He could have heard anything. People are free to say whatever they want to say. And it doesn't necessarily have to be the truth." Taking a pensive sip of her drink, she allowed the thought to take full shape. "What if someone told him I was pushy and always liked to have my way?"

Tom grinned. "Sometimes, you are pushy, but you mean well. And... well, you're usually right."

"I'm afraid we might have judged him harshly. I sure hope not. In my defense and, I might add, to my credit, I made allowances thinking there might have been something in his life, a bad experience or some such thing, which had affected his behavior."

"And what would you say has affected Henrietta's behavior?"

"I couldn't even hazard a guess. By the way, are your cousins allowed to speak freely again?"

"Yes, I thought they might weary of singing Christmas carols so I gave them the rest of the night off."

Clarence cleared his throat and launched into the first line of Hark the Herald Angels Sing.

"I guess I was wrong. Anyhow, have your plans changed?"

"I'm surprised you need to ask. We have a poisoner in our midst. I'm sure the police will eventually get the answers they need to make an arrest. Meanwhile, I don't see any harm in doing what we can to get answers."

CHAPTER 18

Conspiracy of silence

The next morning, Halton House

The pages of the newspaper rustled in quick succession and suddenly stopped. "Lady Woodridge seen entering the schoolhouse."

Evie set her fork down and looked up. She couldn't read Tom's expression because he remained hidden behind the newspaper.

"Is that all it says? Does it describe my outfit? Millicent took great care in selecting it. I think it deserved a mention."

Tom emerged from behind the newspaper long enough to say, "Perhaps the journalist didn't think it important enough to mention details about your clothes in an article about a death in the village."

"I take exception to that. I think it was worthy of some attention. In fact, I don't recall you complimenting me on it."

The Winchester brothers all turned to look at Tom. So far, they hadn't said anything, either because Tom had enforced an embargo on them again or because they actually expected Tom to answer and then Evie to offer a sparring retort. And so on and so forth.

"What else does it say?"

Tom set the newspaper down. "It's vague and brief. They referred to him as a school teacher."

"He was the headmaster."

"Exactly. Facts don't seem to matter. For once, I'd like to read a newspaper and not wonder if what I'm reading is true or made up." Tom looked at his cousins and pushed out a hard breath. "What am I going to do with you lot today?"

"You could send us to the village to spread Christmas cheer," Clarence suggested. "I'm sure the villagers would appreciate our singing."

"That sounds like a marvelous idea," Evie chirped.

"Countess!"

"What? Oh…" Belatedly, Evie remembered the reason for the singing. "I'm sure they've learned their lesson and will keep out of trouble." She turned to the Winchester boys. "Have you learned your lesson?"

"Cousin Evie, do you really need to ask? These are the long suffering faces of contrition."

"Tom, I really don't see the problem. Remember, you wanted to keep them away from the village for fear they might harm Mr. Jackson. Well, he's already dead. There's nothing more they can do. You could go along with them and supervise." Evie stood up. "Anyhow, I must get going. Millicent and I have a full day ahead of us. We'll be back in time for afternoon tea.

On the way out of the dining room, Evie picked up the newspaper and took it with her. When she reached her room, she sat down to read the article.

Tom had been right. The information was sketchy at best and mostly incorrect.

Reading the brief snippet to Millicent, they both shook their heads in disbelief.

"I wonder who gave the reporter that information. Sounds to me like the journalist spoke to a few people and then stitched together an article to fill in some space. They don't even have the day it happened right. Just as well the story is buried in the back pages."

"I wouldn't be surprised if the police provided the information." Setting the newspaper down, she turned her attention to getting herself ready for the rest of the day.

Along the way to meet Mr. Saunders...

"Do you think we should try to have a chat with Anna? She must have seen or heard something. Although, if she had, she would have told the police and since the police didn't mention anything, we have to assume she didn't volunteer any information."

Evie had been reading the letter of recommendation

Mr. Saunders had written. Looking up, she agreed. "But only if we have time after meeting Mrs. Hunter and Mr. Wiltmore. I'm beginning to feel guilty about leaving Mr. Winchester to deal with his cousins by himself."

Half an hour later, Millicent said, "Milady."

"Yes?"

"I'm afraid I have something to confess."

"Confess?" Evie found herself laughing. It had taken the entire night and most of the morning to finally see the humor in Henrietta's attempt to confess to murder.

Thinking Millicent wished to tell her an amusing tale, she said, "You have my full attention."

"I have kept something from you and, in fact, I provided a misleading excuse. Meaning... I actually told a fib. Some people might call it a lie. It wasn't exactly a lie. I'm inclined to think I took some liberties and offered a different interpretation of the truth."

Evie did not dare respond.

"You're shocked. I can tell. You're not even blinking."

Evie blinked. "I'm eager to hear the rest."

"Well, if you recall, yesterday..." Millicent pressed her hand to her chest, almost as if trying to calm herself. "When we returned from the village and found the Winchester lads singing, you then told me to hurry because you needed me to take notes."

Evie nodded.

"And, at first, I did hurry, but then I got caught up reading my notes. That's the lie I told you when I finally went to the drawing room and found you pacing. Do you recall?"

"I do, but I don't understand how it was a lie."

"I used it as an excuse for not coming down straight-away. And, while I did read through my notes…"

"I thought you just said that was a lie."

"Yes, but not really. You see, I did read them but I wasn't reading them just for myself." Millicent closed her eyes and cringed as she pushed the words out, "I read the notes to the Winchester brothers. They wanted to know what we'd found out and since I couldn't remember everything, I had to rely on my notebook and it wasn't enough to summarize it, they wanted to hear everything."

"I see."

"I don't think you, milady. They then wanted to discuss the investigation. So they know every step we took and they know everything we know."

"They're bored, Millicent. And they think what we're doing is exciting."

"You're not mad with me?"

"Are you going to fib to me again?"

"Only if it's absolutely necessary. Meaning, for your own good."

"I hope never to give you reason to feel that way."

"Oh, you never could, milady."

"But you just said… Never mind." They had already driven through several villages and Evie was sure they were close to their destination. When Edmonds slowed down, Evie began paying attention to the buildings in the village they'd just entered.

"This is more like a town, milady."

"The road leads to Bath. It probably benefits from its proximity."

Evie had given Edmonds the address and he was

searching for the landmarks. In the end, he stopped the motor car and stepped out to ask someone.

Mr. Jackson had been employed as a school teacher and the letter of recommendation had exalted his talents for organization and commitment to education.

Evie looked toward the end of the street and could see a building that resembled a school. However, when Edmonds returned, he said Mr. Saunders had retired but the good news was that he lived nearby.

He drove for a few minutes and stopped outside a small manor house.

They saw a gardener sweeping leaves and, when they approached, he tipped his hat and told them Mr. Saunders was indeed home.

Knocking on the front door, they were greeted by an elderly butler with bushy eyebrows who showed them through to a drawing room facing the garden.

Beautifully furnished with quality pieces built to a high standard, Evie noted the lavish upholstery and delightful decorations scattered around the room.

Mr. Saunders appeared at the door, looking quite eager to meet them.

Evie apologized for coming to see him without prior notice and thanked him for making time for them. She wasted no time in explaining their reasons for visiting him.

"Mr. Jackson?"

"Yes, you wrote a letter recommending him for a position as headmaster."

A tall, slim man nearing his fifties and with delicate features, he was dressed in an immaculate dark gray suit with a navy blue tie and black shoes polished to a high sheen.

Mr. Saunders looked lost in thought. Gesturing to a set of chairs, he invited them to sit.

"Of course, Mr. Jackson. How is he?"

"He's met with an accident," Evie said.

"I'm sorry to hear that. When he moved on, we lost contact and I rather hoped everything would work out for him. Has it?"

"Yes. Do you remember being contacted by Mr. Wiltmore."

He gave it some thought. "Wiltmore? The name sounds familiar."

It had only been a relatively short while ago. Evie couldn't imagine him being contacted by a multitude of people asking for character references.

As she studied him, she noticed Mr. Saunders twisting and adjusting his cufflink.

"He would have contacted you in regards to Mr. Jackson's character and experience."

"I see. Yes, of course. Lovely fellow."

The compliment did not sound sincere. In fact, Evie thought he sounded rather nervous.

Evie didn't wish to jump to conclusions, but she couldn't help thinking he would have been an easy target for Mr. Jackson's bullying. Apart from his delicate features, he came across as being quite sensitive.

"Did Mr. Jackson work directly for you?"

"Yes and he did a splendid job running the school. It's a small academy and, I must admit, I inherited the role from a relative who established the school."

"He ran the academy? I thought he'd only taught there."

"Oh, yes. That's right. He did. My apologies. It's been a while since I retired. I only really took it on because it fell on my lap."

None of that made any sense. How could he forget Mr. Jackson had taught at the school? And, it had only been a few months ago.

The butler walked in and drew Mr. Saunders' attention.

After a brief exchange, Mr. Saunders excused himself saying he had some urgent business to attend to.

The butler showed them out and it wasn't until they'd settled into the back seat of the vehicle that Evie managed to find her voice.

"He lied."

Millicent nodded. "And he didn't look comfortable when he heard Mr. Wiltmore's name."

Evie asked Edmonds to drive them to the center of the village where they stopped to have a look around.

"Would you say he was more surprised to hear Mr. Jackson's name or Mr. Wiltmore's name?" Evie asked.

Millicent hummed. "He needed to be reminded about Mr. Jackson and he made a mistake in saying he'd run the school."

It was rare for Evie to regret her actions. In this instance, she had to agree she'd made a mistake. "I wish I'd mentioned the letter to the detective. It just didn't occur to me at the time and, I must admit, even if it had occurred, I might not have told him. The man is infuriating. Still, I do wish I'd thought of it. He might have been able to get more information out of Mr. Saunders. We don't have a badge so we have to rely on the person's willingness to indulge us and, as it turned out, we were shown the door."

"You think he did it deliberately?" Millicent asked.

"I'm certain of it."

They found a tearoom and, because the meeting had been so brief, they decided to kill some time there.

"I wonder if Mr. Jackson came here for his meals." Millicent studied the people at the next table. "Any one of these people here might be acquainted with him. I suppose it would be too awkward to go around asking. Oh, well. It's a pity Mr. Saunders had to rush off. He seemed pleasant and he had a pretty drawing room with lots of decorative pieces. Did you notice the display cabinets? They reminded me of the one Mr. Wiltmore has."

"Are you trying to make some sort of connection?" Evie asked.

"No, I'm just letting my mind wander. It's a good way to generate ideas, but it doesn't always work."

Disappointed with their lack of progress, Evie steered the conversation to the festive season. After having a light meal, they stretched their legs by exploring the village.

"It's a hub of activity," Millicent said and pointed to a wide doorway. "Look at all the business names on that brass plaque."

They walked up to it for a closer look. There were several names but none struck a cord.

Inside, Evie could see a more detailed listing of businesses so they walked in and read through them.

"Mr. Barley, Mr. Peters, Mr. Wiltmore, and Associates," Millicent read. "Could that be a coincidence?"

Evie nodded and read the other listings. They were

quite a few agents for various merchants, a distillery among them, as well as several estate agents.

"It might be worth our while to go in and ask," Evie suggested.

It was a two story building so they walked up to the next floor and found their way to the offices of Mr. Barley and Associates.

A young man behind a desk near the entrance and greeted them. When Evie mentioned Mr. Wiltmore's name on the listing, the young man looked uneasy.

"We've been meaning to remove it for quite some time. He used to be an associate but then he retired."

"When was that?"

"Several years ago. I couldn't really say when. It was definitely before my time."

"What sort of business is this?"

"Solicitors."

Evie tried to remember Mr. Wiltmore's Christian name. She drew out her small notebook and searched through it. "Terence Wiltmore. Would you be able to tell me if it is the same person?"

"As I said, it was before my time."

"It would be greatly appreciated."

While clearly reluctant, the young man excused himself saying he would try to find someone who'd worked there at that time.

When he returned, he asked them to follow them.

Mystified and intrigued, they followed the young man along a wood paneled hallway and were shown through to a large office with leather chairs and a large desk.

A well dressed man with a chain watch hanging from his vest greeted them and introduced himself as Mr.

Barley. He looked to be in his early sixties with graying hair and a cheerful manner. Smiling, he invited them to sit down.

When Evie asked about the name on the listing, he asked them to describe Terence Wiltmore.

Evie did her best and Millicent added a few observations and, between them, they managed to paint a clear enough picture.

"Yes, that's him." The man's tone changed, becoming more reserved. "You say he lives in your village?"

"Yes, he says he's a retired solicitor and he's now a member of the school board."

"I'm sorry to hear that."

Oh, dear…

CHAPTER 19

The Spirit of Christmas

The Village of Woodridge

A scoundrel.

Evie spent the drive back trying to forget what Mr. Barley had told them about Mr. Wiltmore.

They had all been deceived by him. However, on the bright side, she was relieved they had made the trip up to see Mr. Saunders because that had led them to the discovery of the solicitor's office and the truth about Mr. Wiltmore.

"What do we ever really know about anyone?" Evie murmured.

"I assume you want an answer. Let's see. There's Mrs.

Hunter. She loves the company of her cat who looks quite content. She's also fond of a tipple or two."

"I was thinking of Mr. Wiltmore."

"The scoundrel. He enjoys very expensive whiskey and valuable art, all of which he obtained through devious means. He's also known for absconding with clients' belongings and embezzling funds. I'm no longer surprised he can afford to lead an extravagant lifestyle." Millicent frowned. "I still don't understand why they didn't remove his name from the list. I know Mr. Barley explained it, but it still doesn't make sense. Just because he had other clients and they didn't want to lose them. All this time, they've been lying about him having retired. They're as bad as Mr. Wiltmore. Sometimes, I think we value honesty too much. If we didn't, we wouldn't be constantly surprised by what people do and say."

Evie looked out the window at the passing scenery. She would have to present this information to the detective. But what did it prove and would he welcome the information or would he accuse her of meddling in police business?

There had to be some other connection.

Evie gasped.

"What is it?"

"We do have a connection."

"To what?"

"A connection between Mr. Wiltmore and Mr. Jackson." Evie realized it couldn't be a coincidence that they'd both lived in the same village.

"What is it?"

Evie stilled. "Oh, dear. I had it. Now it's gone."

"Where?"

"Gone, as in, one moment it was clear and now it's not."

"How long has Mr. Wiltmore lived in the village?" Millicent asked.

"Three or four years."

"There's the connection." Instead of explaining, Millicent straightened and pointed ahead. "Look, it's the Winchester lads and they've drawn a crowd."

"That's the connection?"

"No, I'm just drawing your attention to your cousins. I think they're singing. How do you think they escaped the house?"

Evie realized she'd forgotten to tell Millicent about it. "They have Mr. Winchester's permission."

Millicent laughed. "He let them out for good behavior?"

Evie leaned in and narrowed her eyes. "Is that the detective with them?"

Millicent leaned forward and asked Edmonds to stop. Sitting back, she asked, "Did you want to stop and talk to him?"

"And say what?"

"Anything that will make him speak with Mr. Saunders and get more information out of him. I'm sure he knows something. And the detective might be able to see the connection you think is there."

They both lived in the same village.

Evie closed her eyes. If they hadn't gone for a walk, they would not have seen the brass plaque with the business names or been drawn to the more detailed list inside the building.

"What if Mr. Jackson had the same experience?"

Seeing Millicent's puzzled expression, Evie explained her thought process.

"Yes, that must be it. Mr. Jackson must have known something about Mr. Wiltmore and… and he followed him here."

"And then?" Evie asked.

Instead of answering, Millicent pointed to the detective. "Let him figure it out."

Evie and Millicent climbed out of the motor car. However, they then hesitated.

"Are we going to sound like raving lunatics?" Evie asked.

"There's only one way to find out."

The moment the detective saw them, he began walking toward them.

"Lady Woodridge and Miss Peters."

"Detective. It's good to see you embracing the festive season."

"Yes, I must admit, I've been greatly entertained while waiting for you."

"Me?"

He nodded. "It seems you have come across a vital piece of information which you failed to bring to my attention."

"Me?"

He nodded again.

"Rumor has it you are in possession of a letter."

"Where did you hear that?"

Millicent spluttered, "Anna. It has to be Anna. She had just brought in the tea and she must have lingered by the door. She is the source of all this information getting around."

Evie dug inside her handbag and produced the letter. However, before she handed it to the detective, she told him about Mr. Saunders and Mr. Barley. Then, drawing in a deep breath, she told him about Mr. Wiltmore.

"Embezzlement?"

Evie nodded. "And extortion. He would get anything from valuable paintings to cases of fine Scotch whiskey. Mr. Wiltmore is rather fond to it too. My cousins can attest to that."

The detective stilled.

"What is it?"

"The autopsy revealed large amounts of whiskey." He looked into the distance.

"Are you saying that's how he was poisoned?"

He nodded.

"Detective, you should arrest Mr. Wiltmore now and ask questions later," Millicent declared.

CHAPTER 20

Merry Christmas

Christmas Tree trimming
The hall, Halton House

"Mr. Jackson was both a villain and a hero," Henrietta mused. "I find that hard to believe. I never met the man, but it seems contradictory. You can be one or the other, but not both. I'm sure of it."

Sarah smiled. "I beg to differ, Henrietta."

"Why am not surprised, Sarah. Do share."

"Well, you have your moments of clarity and then you go off on one of your madhouse antics. And, by the way, I found the perfect spot for your portrait up in the gallery with all the other dowagers."

"Perfect, do make sure to reserve a place for yourself."

"How strange," Toodles said. "I suddenly feel left out."

"Oh, no. We can't have that, my dear. We'll give you an honorary spot," Henrietta offered. "We'll have to arrange to have your portrait painted. If I'm not mistaken, Lady Evans' mother in law paints portraits."

Caro, Lady Evans, looked at Evie and laughed.

Yes, indeed, however, her mother in law had a penchant for painting nude paintings.

"Caro, dear. Do you think your dear mother in law would be amenable to the idea of doing a portrait of Toodles?" Henrietta gave Toodles a warm smile. "I'm sure she'll slim you down if you ask nicely."

Caro leaned in and whispered, "Does Henrietta actually require an answer?"

"No, she's just having fun at Toodles' expense." Smiling, Evie invited Caro to tell her everything she'd left out in her letters.

"Oh, but I want to hear all about Mr. Jackson. Henry doesn't like talking about his cases and I find myself missing the excitement."

"There's nothing exciting about stumbling on a dead body."

"No, but then you made the connection. How did you do that?"

Evie had been wondering about that. "I think I wanted to prove something. I just didn't want to believe Mr. Jackson had always been rude. So I set out to have a chat with one of the people who wrote a letter of recommendation. I'm afraid I didn't get very far with him. When we mentioned Mr. Jackson, he didn't get his facts right and that triggered alarm bells. There just seemed something odd about forgetting something that had happened only recently."

Detective Inspector Everett had eventually succeeded in getting more information out of Mr. Saunders who'd admitted to being coerced by Mr. Jackson to write the letter.

"So he'd wanted the position in the village school because he'd discovered Mr. Wiltmore lived here."

"Yes. One of Mr. Jackson's relatives had been a victim of Mr. Wiltmore's embezzling schemes. By the time Mr. Jackson found out, Mr. Wiltmore had left the village. Or, rather, he'd been forced out by his associates who'd opted to avoid a scandal by not bringing charges."

"And Mr. Jackson eventually traced him here."

Evie nodded. "Everything fell into place for him. The position at the school opened up and he set out to coerce Mr. Saunders into writing a glowing reference letter."

"That's the part I don't understand." Caro shook her head. "Why didn't he contact the authorities?"

On the one hand, Mr. Jackson had been a hero because he'd located Mr. Wiltmore. They could only guess at his intentions. However, somewhere along the line, he'd turned into a villain. "Instead of alerting the authorities, he set out to make Mr. Wiltmore pay for his crimes."

Detective Inspector Everett had forced a confession out of Mr. Wiltmore, who'd tried to portray himself as the victim because Mr. Jackson had blackmailed him.

"And then Mr. Jackson became the victim. Did Mr. Wiltmore really think he would get away with poisoning him?"

"He must have. He very nearly did but now he's behind

bars." Evie handed Caro a bright red bauble, a Halton House tradition with everyone getting to hang one on the tree. At least, that was the intention, but Henrietta was in charge of selecting where the baubles should hang, so they'd been waiting a while.

"Down a fraction. Now a bit to the right. No… I meant the left. Don't mind me. I'm distracted by the dazzling display. It is a delightful tree."

They all stood around the tree, with everyone holding Christmas tree decorations and waiting patiently for Henrietta to call their name.

"I'm so glad you came in time for the Christmas pageant. The children are excited to be doing something fun. We had to draw straws for the roles of Mole, Rat and their loopy friend, Toad. Seth will be arriving soon, so he'll also be able to attend." Evie had planned on driving with Tom to collect the young Earl of Woodridge from school, but then Caro had arrived and Phillipa Brady had telephoned from London to say she would be on the late afternoon train. So Tom had driven off by himself.

The thought lingered in her mind even as the front door opened and Tom walked in with Seth charging ahead and chasing Holmes.

Caro smiled. "I still think young Seth is too young to be in boarding school."

Evie laughed.

"Just in time to trim the tree," Tom said as he joined them, his eyes bright with enthusiasm. "Edmonds is coming up the drive with Phillipa and Henry. They were both on the same train. We saw them as we were driving through the village."

"How wonderful," Evie said as all the servants arrived to participate in decorating the tree.

Then Brazen and Wilbur began singing and everyone joined in, "Deck the halls with boughs of holly…"

***

Printed in Great Britain
by Amazon